HOUSE OF STOCKHOLM

Amy Elizabeth

Amy Elizabeth is a Welsh author raised by the sea, where wild tides and weather-beaten cliffs first taught her about beauty, defiance, and the stories that hide beneath the surface. Her fiction lingers at the crossroads of love and justice, exploring what it means to be a woman beneath the weight of expectation — and what happens when that weight is finally cast off. Her work explores womanhood, power, and moral defiance against the shadowed backdrop of patriarchal society.

Drawing inspiration from the lyricism of the Brontës, the emotional depth of Thomas Hardy, and the intensity of modern fantasy authors such as Sarah J. Maas, her writing bridges gothic tradition with contemporary resonance — weaving beauty, rage, and resilience into every line.

House of Stockholm is her debut novel. She is currently at work on its sequel, continuing the haunting tale of love, justice, and reclamation.

To all who dream of escape.

Chapter One

Rain slid down the carriage window in fine silver threads, trembling each time the wheels struck a rut in the road. Beyond the glass, the sea lay vast and grey, its waves hurling themselves against the cliffs with the violence of beasts. Once, I had loved the sea; today it seemed intent upon swallowing me whole.

"Tabitha, you're hogging the window again." That was Beatrice, my eldest sister by four years, her voice sharpened with the authority she wore like a crown. "Move over."

"I am not hogging," I protested, though I knew full well I was. I edged back an inch, just enough for her to press her gloved fingers against the misted glass.

"Mother will not like it if we arrive bedraggled," Lydia murmured from across the seat, smoothing a wrinkle from her pale blue skirts. Always the peacemaker, she spoke softly, as though gentleness itself might mend the flaws of the world.

"Mother will not like anything," Clara said tartly, dark hair glinting in the dim light, eyes quick with mischief. "She will find fault, as she always does."

"Clara." Beatrice snapped her name like a whip, though Clara only smirked and crossed her ankles with deliberate elegance.

Beside me, little Marianne tugged the ribbon of her bonnet, cheeks flushed with excitement. "I do not care what Mother likes. We are going to Marrowhall House. Do you know what they say? That its floors are of marble, its chandeliers cut from Venetian glass, its gallery is said to rival the very tapestries of Delphi. And there are red rooms—like in the palaces on the Continent." Her eyes sparkled. She was young enough still to believe such tales.

"Red rooms?" Clara arched a brow.

"What need has anyone for red rooms, unless to hide some ghastly crime?" Lydia gasped softly.

"Clara!"

I smiled despite myself. That was Clara's gift — to lace shadows into the ordinary, to say aloud the thing we all half-thought but would never dare voice.

The sea wind howled through the seams of the carriage, raising gooseflesh upon my arms. My thoughts strayed homeward, to Wales: Father, bent over his books in silence, the air of his study thick with pipe smoke; Mother, brittle and scornful, her voice slicing walls as cleanly as glass. Ours was a house of comfort, of inherited land and stone, but not of status. It was not enough for Mother. She longed to see us lifted higher, married into fortune and name. That was why we had accepted the invitation to Marrowhall House. For her, it was not an afternoon of pleasantry but a ladder, one rung closer to escape from mediocrity.

"Tabby's dreaming again," Marianne sang, her tone lilting.

"Look at her face—she is always dreaming."

Heat rushed to my cheeks.

"I am not."

"You are," Clara said slyly. "Always staring at the sea as though it might answer you. What is it you want, Tabitha?

Adventure? Escape? A husband?" A tone with an intended likeness to my mother's.

"Not a husband, Mother!" I said quickly. They all laughed, even Lydia with her soft, secret smile. Beatrice only shook her head.

"You will have to marry someday, Tabitha. You cannot float forever with your head in the clouds. But as the carriage thundered on and the waves surged beside us, I thought perhaps I could. Perhaps the clouds were the only place left to breathe. My gaze drifted seaward, to the restless silver crests, and without willing it, memory carried me back—I was a young girl. It was midsummer on the Welsh Coast, the air thick with salt and gull cries. My sisters knelt in the sand, Beatrice commanding us to fetch seawater for her moat. I wandered further, drawn by a shell glimmering pink in a tidepool.

The tide rose unnoticed until the ground fell away beneath my feet and the sea swallowed me whole. The world turned green and endless. My limbs flailed, lungs burned, but a strange calm stole over me. The current wrapped me like arms, the surface gleamed just beyond reach, and I thought, only for a heartbeat, that I belonged to the sea.

Even now, the memory sent a shiver down my spine.

"Tabitha." Beatrice's voice yanked me back. Her hand covered mine, where I clutched the seat too tightly. "You are pale. Are you unwell?"

"I am quite well," I lied, folding my hands neatly. But outside, the waves crashed mockingly, as though they whispered: you are mine, and one day you will return.

Chapter Two

The carriage wheels shrieked as they descended, iron rims biting into gravel. The storm had passed, leaving the world scoured bright. Blue spread across the sky, scrubbed clean by rain, sunlight breaking into glittering shards upon the sea.

"Are we nearly there?" Marianne leaned half out of the window, bonnet ribbons whipping.

"At last," Lydia soothed, dabbing condensation from the glass with her handkerchief. "Look."

Marrowhall House rose from the cliffside like some conjuration. All pale marble and cream stone, its façade caught the sun as though it had been waiting for the light. Columns too pristine for this rough Cornish coast flanked its entrance, streaked faintly red where iron gutters had bled rust. Above, a central dome glimmered.

"Marble," Marianne whispered.

"Cream," Lydia corrected gently.

"And red," Clara said with relish. "Blood shows brightest on pale stone."

Beatrice glared. "Clara, hush."

But Clara only smiled, her eyes daring the Hall itself to listen. I said nothing. To me, the windows seemed black and watchful, like eyes that did not blink. The sea roared beneath, booming in rhythm with my own heart.

We slowed at last before the steps. Servants moved forward, blank-faced in their livery, hands outstretched in empty courtesy. My skirts brushed damp gravel as I stepped down. Sunlight danced on marble, too bright to bear. Above us the great oak door swung open, spilling golden light. A woman stood framed there, her gown of Emerald hues blazing against the pale façade.

"Welcome to Marrowhall House" she said smoothly.

My sisters dipped their curtsies, voices mingling. I bent low as well, though my eyes slid past her, drawn to the great house that loomed like the sea itself.

The reception was a cathedral of light and colour. Cream walls draped with crimson velvet; a gilded ceiling painted with cherubs, whose baby-blue robes echoed the shade of my own dress. Their faces grinned too sweetly, their eyes too round, as though mocking rather than blessing. In the drawing room, a fire roared; its smoke scented faintly of resin and oak, heat licking at crystal and mirrored sconces until the room shimmered like a jewel box. Silver glinted on the tea table, beside cakes lacquered with sugared glaze and sandwiches cut with cruel precision.

I entered behind my sisters, awkward in my own skin. My dress — a pale blue thing puffed at the sleeves, girlish and unflattering — chosen by mother of course. I had caught sight of myself in the glass before we left: the hairstyle did nothing for my face, only made me look narrow and plain. It had been scraped into plaits wound too tight beneath a bonnet that itched and pinched my scalp. Fitting though, as no light ever reflected off the dull, fawn tones from my scalp — it had no shine to parade. Better hidden away, quite like myself. No paint touched my cheeks. No powder softened my paleness. I was exactly as I had been made — untouched, unshaped, unknowing.

It was all by design. My mother believed innocence a currency, ignorance a weapon. Let the world see us as modest, pliant, and ready to be moulded into wives. That was why we were here; we had not come to Marrowhall simply for tea.

We then took our seats.

The lady who presided at the head of the table, her gown gleaming stiffly, her smile practiced. She poured tea with hands that never wavered.

"Such a blessing to have young company," she said, her tone smooth.

"We are most grateful for your invitation," Beatrice answered quickly, already playing her part as eldest. She reached for the sugar tongs at the same moment as Clara, their hands colliding.

"Do go on, Bea," Clara said, her smile too sweet. "You must always lead."

Beatrice's nostrils flared, but she swallowed her retort, dropping a cube of sugar into her cup as though setting down a challenge.

Lydia sighed. "Must we quarrel over sugar?"

"Better sugar than husbands," Clara murmured.

I hid a smile behind my teacup. Marianne, meanwhile, had drawn a small leather-bound book from her reticule — a dictionary.

"Marianne," Beatrice hissed. "Put that away."

"I like words," she said, her eyes bright. "Listen to this one. Stockholm syndrome."

Lydia blinked. "Wherever did you—"

"It says," Marianne read aloud, "'A condition in which a captive comes to feel affection for their captor.'"

"A foolish woman, then," Clara said lightly. "Or one with no other choice."

A silence pressed down, thick as velvet, as though even the painted cherubs on the ceiling leaned in to listen. I busied myself with my teacup, but the word echoed in me: captive, captor, affection.

❖

I excused myself to powder my nose and the words felt flimsy the moment I spoke them. It was the best lie I had: a small vanity no one could doubt, an excuse to steal away from the polite laughter and the brittle compliments of the drawing room. My sisters barely noticed me slip from the circle of their voices; they were occupied with the pastries and with each other, and Marrowhall's light made them bright and careless.

A footman inclined his head when I passed, as if guiding me to the nearest retiring-room, and pointed vaguely down a corridor. I followed the direction he had given, but the great house was more labyrinth than map. Marble halls opened into salons, into libraries heavy with dust, into small oratories with painted saints who watched me with eyes that seemed to ask questions I had no answers for. Sunlight lay like a sheet across the upper floors, the cream stone glowing warm and almost holy. It was only when I ventured farther, chasing the idea of a hidden closet or a mirror unoccupied, that the light thinned and shadows gathered. I took one passage after another until the house's civility thinned beneath my feet. The marble suddenly gave way to rougher stone, the air cooling, thickening with the scent of wax and something sweeter, more clinging. Each door I passed tightened the quiet like a breath held too long.

At the end of the stair, I found a narrow corridor, its walls hung with tapestries whose threads had once been bright but now dulled with secrets. Doors stood like closed mouths. From them came sounds that stung: muffled laughter, a woman's soft moan, the scrape of heels on rugs. I should have turned then. Instead, curiosity — a poor, greedy thing — tugged me forward.

The first room I saw was drained of daylight, its velvet drapes swallowing the sun. Masks hung on pegs like trophies: birds, beasts, faces whose smiles were painted too wide. On a low chaise a woman reclined in rouge and silk, her hair tumbled, a man at her side whispering. Their faces were hidden; their hands moved in ways I understood but had never seen in truth. I stepped back, and another door sighed open as if excited to show me its own corruption.

A chamber of candles: men in half-masks watched a woman dance upon a chair, skirts flaring, coins flashing as they were thrown. Another cavity in the hallway held a tableau of robes and ropes, jewelled collars and leather straps laid out like implements on a dresser. The things were arranged with the neatness of ritual. My skin prickled. I pressed my fingers to my mouth to keep from crying out. The world above — the music, the clinking china, the polite small talk — felt a long way off, as though someone had cut the house in two and sealed me into the underside.

At the corridor's end I found a room that might have been a costume chest: feathered cloaks, sequined bodices, masks inlaid with glass that caught the candlelight and fractured it into small knives. I could not help myself; I touched one mask. Cold lacquer met my fingertips and for a moment I imagined what it would be to wear such a thing, to be someone else entirely.

"Ah, a little bird has fallen from its nest."

The voice came close enough to cool the air around me. I trembled so violently that the mask in my hand rattled against the table. I turned and saw him step from the shadow: a man whose height filled the doorway, the half-mask he wore black as a raven's wing. The corridor narrowed and his shadow seemed to swallow the candlelight. He moved with a confidence I had not seen among the other staff. Before I could find my voice, he reached for my skirts. His fingers closed on the fabric with a strength that made me gasp. In that instant, the candlelight caught on the ring upon his finger — heavy, gold, the face of a wolf cast in profile, teeth bared in a perpetual snarl.

The metal reflected the flame and the wolf's eyes seemed alive, hungry and cunning.

The sight of it drew a sharp breath from me. I did not know the man; I did not know his intentions. I only knew that the ring, small and awful on his hand, belonged to a creature that hunted by pack and by guile. I wrenched free, the fabric tearing where his grip had been, and fled. The corridor blurred; doors creaked open and hands reached from within as if the rooms themselves were reluctant to lose their spectator. His footsteps pounded after me, quick and precise, the sound of pursuit. I ran until my calves burned, until the stair turned and I found a window thrown wide to the day.

I remember the sunlight — such sunlight as had gleamed on the marble above, now a thin blade searing past the muddied glass. My skirts snagged on the sill; a servant's hand grazed my sleeve. For one ridiculous second, I thought of my sisters, of Beatrice's scorn, of Lydia's patient face. Then I clambered, throwing myself into the air. The sea yawned and the world overturned. Cold struck like iron. I felt the wind ripped from me, the salt filling my mouth. For a moment I cursed silently at the sea for taking me, for the cruelty of its depths. Then—strangely—the panic dulled. The current wrapped around me as it had once before when I was a child, and though I flailed, a part of me surrendered to the darkness as if it were a warm cloak.

Chapter Three

I awoke choking, my chest heaving as brine spilled from my lips. For a dreadful instant I believed I was still in the sea's grasp, tumbling in its black coils. But when my vision steadied, I beheld plaster above me, pale and unadorned, and the wavering glow of lamplight upon a low ceiling. I was not drowning. I was sprawled upon a velvet chaise; my garments sodden, my hair heavy as rope against my shoulders.

"You are alive." The voice was clear, deliberate. I turned my head and found a woman standing over me. She was tall, commanding, her gown of deep burgundy drawn close to a narrow waist. Her dark eyes, sharp as cut glass, surveyed me with the detachment of one accustomed to judgment. She wrung seawater from a folded cloth with hands that did not tremble.

I struggled to sit, but my limbs failed me. At once, she pressed me back with a touch that brooked no refusal.

"Be still. You were found upon the rocks below the cliff. The tide would not have spared you another hour."

My throat was raw; each word rasped like sand.

"Where am I?"

"Penryn House," she replied. "My home. I am Lady Hawthorne." The name held no meaning for me, yet her bearing commanded reverence. She studied me as though I were a curiosity brought in from the sea. "And you are?"

I opened my lips, but no sound came. My thoughts fled to my sisters, to the bright morning that now felt an age past. Panic seized me. I tried again to rise.

"Tabitha. I—I must return—my sisters—"

"No." The single syllable cracked like a whip in the stillness. She stepped closer, her presence filling the chamber. "You will not return. You cannot. Whatever you stumbled upon within the walls of Marrowhall, those who dwell there will not suffer you to live, should they learn you escaped."

Her gaze did not waver. "You must understand me: you died today. The sea claimed you, and the world must believe it so. To speak your name again is to invite death."

The words struck me with greater force than the waves had. "But who am I, if not myself?" I whispered, scarcely able to breathe. She lowered herself until her shadow fell across me, her hand firm upon mine.

"You will become someone else. A guest of good breeding, brought here beneath my patronage. You shall be—" She paused for a brief moment, "—*Alexandra*." The name—Alexandra—hung in the air, unfamiliar, sharp as a blade. A stranger's name. Yet as I whispered it, I felt something shift within me, as though the tide had stripped away one life and left another in its place.

"Let it be your shield, your disguise. Behind it, you may yet walk unmarked. Without it, you will be hunted." Lady Hawthorne's expression then gradually softened, though her tone did not. Her eyes held mine, steady, deliberate.

"Within these walls, you will be as a goddaughter to me. Penryn shall offer you its shelter. I will see to it that you are taught as befits a young woman of standing—your manners, your education, your bearing. You will learn what it is to move through the world as more than prey."

A knot rose in my throat.

"But...why?" The question escaped before I could stop it. "Why such care for me? I am nothing to you."

Lady Hawthorne's gaze softened only slightly, but enough to unsettle me.

"Because the world does not forgive women easily. Do not look backward child."

The fire crackled in the grate, casting long shadows that climbed the walls. I stared into them, and something within me hardened.

Tabitha had drowned.

❖

In the dim chamber, Lady Hawthorne brought me vials, herbs, and bark, their sharp scents rising in coils that filled my lungs until I could taste the bitterness on my tongue. She bade me grind and mix them with my own hands, the mortar groaning under the weight of roots and powders. The paste bled rust-red across my fingertips, clinging like dried blood. The bark clung to the edge of the bowl like tar. When I worked it through my hair, the sting flared against my scalp, sharper than saltwater, biting until my eyes watered. The acrid tang of it seeped into my throat, burning deeper than the sea had, as though I were being remade from the marrow outward.

"Beauty and womanhood come at a dear price", my sister once told me. Now, at last, I understood. Pain is the toll exacted at every threshold. When I first bled at fourteen, the shame and terror was unbearable. No one had warned me; no one had told me that my own body would betray me so. I remembered the panic, the tears swallowed down, the desperate silence. Blood on my hands, for a crime I never knew I'd committed.

I remembered my eldest sister took me aside. In hushed tones she explained the truth — that womanhood is a bargain, struck not by us but by God and the Devil themselves; the highest of patriarchs seated at their table, declaring at the beginning of time itself that females should be the currency to life.

"To thrive, you must endure," she whispered, her eyes old before their time. "To survive, you must suffer. That is the price." I had not understood then. I did now.

The blue of my sodden dress, puffed and shapeless, was stripped away. Its girlish folds, which had hidden me rather than revealed me, now lay discarded upon the floor, as limp and lifeless as the girl I had been. With it went the jewels I had once prized — delicate, flimsy trinkets, gifts of affection but not of lineage, baubles without story. They were weightless, and so I cast them aside.

Lady Hawthorne arrayed me instead in a gown of burgundy silk that seemed to drink in the lamplight. It clung to me as if it already knew me, the lace curling across my form in dark, intricate patterns, like veins of shadow on pale stone. Around my throat she fastened a pendant, heavy as truth, pressing into my collarbone with the solemn weight of protection — or of claim. It felt purposeful, almost regal, as though it had been waiting for me.

When at last I dared raise my gaze to the mirror, I scarcely knew the reflection staring back. The hair I had spent years subduing — pinned flat, straightened, hidden — now cascaded unrestrained, a storm of curls about my shoulders. The dye had transformed it into a dark mahogany, yet in the lamplight it glowed with living fire: hues of molten garnet shimmering as though embers smouldered beneath each strand. In shadow it deepened into raven-black, lustrous and severe. By candlelight it caught hints of copper, fleeting sparks of red like wine poured over flame. The shifting hues made it a crown that changed with every breath of light.

The curls sculpted my cheekbones, lifted the hollows of my face, so that my pallor no longer seemed the pallor of the drowned but of porcelain — rare, luminous, untouchable. My eyes, green as sea-glass, burned brighter now, framed by the darkness above them. My freckles, once the marks of girlhood, shone instead like constellations across a new sky.

The girl I had been was gone. The mirror showed only a woman — sharpened, remade, claimed. From head to toe, I was no longer the drowned girl upon the rocks. I was someone else entirely.

Alexandra.

Chapter Four

The morning light in Penryn House was different to what I was accustomed to back home—quieter, as though filtered through time itself. It spilled across the wooden floorboards of my chamber with a kind of composure I had never known.

The house stirred slowly. Somewhere below, I heard the clatter of pans in the kitchen and the distant crow of a rooster echoing across the green. I rose, the coolness of the stone floor meeting my bare feet, and crossed to the window. Mist clung to the fields beyond the orchard, silvering the garden paths and the tops of hedgerows. From this height, Penryn looked less like a house and more like a haven.

A gentle knock came at the door. Before I could answer, it opened an inch and Lady Hawthorn's voice followed it in.

"I trust you slept well?"

She entered without waiting for permission, though not unkindly. There was a briskness to her manner, a woman well-accustomed to managing people and rooms.

"Well enough, thank you," I replied, smoothing the edge of the coverlet.

"Good. There's breakfast waiting—modest, but sufficient. Please join me when you are ready."

I offered a polite smile.

Lady Hawthorn sat at the small writing chair near the hearth and folded her hands atop her lap.

"We are not idle here at Penryn," Lady Hawthorne said at last, her voice soft but lined with steel. "The mornings are best reserved for the cultivation of feminine discipline. A lady ought to rise early, practice her scales, refine her painting, her needlework… even posture. One's bearing says more than one's bloodline, in the end."

She looked me over—not unkindly, but with a measuring sort of gaze.

"If you feel certain refinements were overlooked in your education, I could have a governess arranged. Just for a time." I drew my shawl tighter around my shoulders, though the room was warm.

"That won't be necessary," I replied, not impolitely, but firm. I chose not to elaborate further. But inside, my mother's voice stirred — brisk and clear as cut glass:

"A house runs best when all hands find something useful to do."

There had never been a governess back home. No daily instruction in embroidery or correct conversational French. And yet, my mother ensured there was balance. Between the kneading of bread and the mending of hems, she taught us to read, to speak with care, to sit tall and walk straight. Manners were not drilled, but absorbed — not only to impress, but to uphold one's dignity.

So that's what I had always done. And what I still longed to do. Not to become just a lady, but something tangible. Something capable.

I looked back at Lady Hawthorne and offered a soft smile —one that said nothing, and everything.

She gave a small nod, part satisfied. "Well, I've arranged for a girl to assist you either way. She'll serve as both maid and chaperone, should the need arise. She is quiet, efficient, and punctual. I think you'll find her agreeable."

She turned her head toward the door. "Una?"

A figure entered then—taller, perhaps a few years older than myself, though she carried herself with the composure of someone twice that. There was a gravity to her—as though something not entirely of this world had stepped into mine, a sentinel cloaked in plain cloth and purpose.

Her chestnut hair was bound neatly at the nape, and though she wore no jewellery nor finery, there was something striking in her bearing. She offered a small curtsy, eyes lifted but guarded.

"Miss Greystone, this is Una. She'll see that your linen is kept fresh, your appointments remembered, and your space well managed."

I inclined my head. "Thank you, Una."

She said nothing, but her expression shifted—just slightly. Something between acknowledgment and quiet approval.

Lady Hawthorn stood. "I leave you in good hands."

And with that, she swept from the room, her presence fading like the perfume of dried lavender behind her.

Una remained a moment longer, then moved silently to the side table to adjust the candle. When she passed by me, I caught a faint scent of lemon and starch, and something else—something clean and rooted. She did not speak, but I thought I saw the edge of a smile.

❖

I dressed with Una's quiet assistance. At her suggestion, I exchanged the silk and lace for something more sensible—a soft cotton day dress in a slate blue, with a hem that brushed just above my ankles. A simple choice, the sort worn by women who expect to move with purpose rather than be admired. She braided my hair back from my face in a single plait and pinned it neatly.

"You'll want a shawl, Miss." Una said at last, her first words of the morning, offered as she folded one across my arm. "The stones don't warm until mid-afternoon."

I offered a quiet thank you. She nodded once and disappeared through the side door.

Outside my chamber, the air carried the faint scent of beeswax and stone. I descended the main staircase slowly. The stairs curved in twin flights from opposite ends of the upper gallery, like two ribbons of carved oak unfurling toward one another. They met at a single landing, then descended together in a broad, sweeping stair that spilled into the main corridor below. The balustrades were heavy with age, their spindles hand-turned and polished by decades of palms now gone. Each step creaked faintly underfoot — not enough to startle, but enough to remind one of all who had walked there before.

As I took each step, Penryn unfolded before me.

Above, the gallery ran like a spine through the heart of the house, lined with portraits in oil and gilt, their painted eyes ever-watchful. Below, the corridor stretched long and hushed, its black-and-white tiles catching what light could reach through the tall windows by the door. It was not a staircase made to be climbed in haste — but one to descend with measured step, as though carrying the weight of a name.

The wood beneath my feet was pale oak, softened at the edges by age. More portraits lined the walls—none grand, none familiar. A gentle hush lingered in the corners, as though the house preferred silence. Its strength lay in stillness.

The drawing room, passed through only briefly, held the hush of unused parlours: a faint scent of lavender sachet, sun-faded drapes pulled back by simple cords, a hearth swept clean. A pastoral painting hung above the mantel— two cows near a riverbank, rendered with more affection than skill. The furniture was worn but cared for, the rugs faded from sunlight, the cushions slightly uneven as though someone had just risen from them and would return shortly.

In the passage that led to the kitchen, the smells were richer—yeast, toasted oats, something buttery and crisp. The cook, a stout woman with rosy cheeks and sleeves rolled to the elbow, was elbow-deep in flour. She glanced up only once, and though she said nothing, her eyes said much. I nodded politely and moved on.

I paused in the music room. A smaller space tucked to the rear of the house. It faced the gardens and caught the pale light like a bowl catching raindrops. I sat at the piano, its varnish dulled by years and fingertips. The keys responded with soft resistance, a breath of sound. I played a few notes—fragments of melodies half-remembered—and let the silence answer me in kind.

When I stepped outside, the world opened like a page turned carefully. Penryn sat cradled in the arms of a green valley, the hills folding round it like protective wings. The garden paths were gravelled and moss-laced, leading past low stone walls furred with lichen. Wildflowers tangled across arched trellises; it was like walking through a kaleidoscope. The scent of wet earth lingered from the morning's mist, and somewhere nearby, a trickle of a babbling brook sang in long, continuous rhythm. Runner ducks toddled indignantly through a crooked gate, their feet slapping the path. Chickens scattered like Autumn leaves in wind at my approach, their feathers ruffled, eyes bright with suspicion.

By midday, my sleeves were streaked with earth and my cheeks flushed from the sun. I followed a worn path past the outbuildings—weathered barns and a henhouse roofed in rusted tin—until I found the basket and gathered the eggs, warm and heavy in my palms like small suns.

Further along, near the lily pond, a terrier the colour of storm-clouds darted through the underbrush. He stopped just long enough to let me scratch behind his ears, then bolted after some imagined enemy, tail high with purpose.

From a distance, I caught the eyes of two maids near the scullery door. One watched me with narrowed interest, the other whispered behind her hand. A groom passed me near the orchard wall, doffing his cap but saying nothing. They were puzzled, perhaps, or simply unaccustomed to mistresses who plucked eggs and carried baskets like any servant.

But as I passed Una, who stood near the pump with a folded sheet in her arms, I caught a flicker of expression. Not quite a smile—something softer.

Something noted.

She had the kind of eyes that judged, but with ears that truly listened, compassionately. Though she spoke little, I felt it — that fierce, unwavering presence of sincerity.

By the time I returned to my room, the light had begun to wane. Evening crept slowly through the valley, trailing shadows like ink poured into water. The house had grown quiet, its corners darker, its silences longer. Penryn did not roar at night—it withdrew, like a creature folding in on itself for rest.

I removed the dress that I'd changed into for dinner— nothing elaborate, only a gown of deep plum wool, its sleeves gathered modestly at the wrists, the collar edged with black lace. The fabric was heavy yet comforting. A layer of delicate protection. The candle Una had lit earlier still flickered on the vanity, its flame dancing faintly in the looking-glass. I crossed the room and sat before it; oval shaped and clouded at the edges, the silver behind it tarnished with age. Una had left a clean chemise; I slipped it over my shoulders. The silk fell like the sigh of the sea, cool against my skin, clinging where it wished as though the fabric itself had drawn breath.

I loosened my hair and ran the soft-bristled brush through its length, each stroke slow and deliberate. Stray curls slipped free, falling across my shoulders like threads of twilight. I watched myself in the mirror, not with vanity, but with something nearer to mourning.

The chamber was moody, but not cold. The walls were painted in a rich maroon. Thick velvet curtains— burgundy, near to wine, hung heavy at the window. They muffled the wind, holding the night at bay. A four-poster bed stood against the far wall, its frame carved from dark wood, the gauze drapes replaced here with fine damask that shimmered faintly where the candlelight touched it. The linens were embroidered in gold thread, the pillows edged with lace. The vanity I was seated at stood opposite the bed in regal stillness, its surface scattered with small, thoughtful luxuries: a crystal bottle of lavender water, a carved silver brush moulded in my palm, a mirror framed in ivy latticework. Everything was subdued, but rich. Everything chosen sensibly, with purpose.

There were no gas lamps in Penryn, no polished brass. But the room breathed with quiet wealth, the sort that whispers rather than boasts. One shuttered window overlooked the garden, where the moon hung pale above the lily pond, its reflection broken by the soft ripple of a breeze across water. At the other end, a tree's branches endlessly brushing like whispering sisters.

I missed them—My sisters, Mother and Father, with a sudden, aching intensity. I had not allowed myself to feel it today—not while the sun was high, not while my hands were busy with soil, straw and basket. But now, in the hush of evening, it settled around me like a shroud of sorrow.

Was I among their thoughts? Did they feel my absence as I felt theirs? I did not know. I only knew that I could not reach for them—not yet. Not while the suffocating dust still hung in the air. One day, perhaps. When the world had quieted. When I could return not as the girl who flees, but as a woman who fights. Unbound, unshackled from the burdens laid upon me.

The door creaked softly.

Una entered, her arms full of fresh linen, folded neatly. She did not speak, only moved about the room with her usual quiet efficiency. The scent of lavender followed her. She paused at the edge of the room, her voice low and even.

"Shall I run you a bath, Miss?"

I met her gaze in the mirror and gave a small, grateful nod. "Yes, please, Una. Thank you."

Chapter Five

The town market lay scattered like a quilt across the cobbled square, each stall a patch of colour and scent sewn into the grey morning. Sea-mist drifted low along the harbour, veiling the hills in pale gauze. Its hum was much softer than a city—less clamour, more murmur. The people moved with the quiet dignity of those accustomed to wind, salt and sky. Baskets of winter apples nestled beside jars of treacle and lavender honey. Bolts of wool, thick and ochre-dyed, hung behind a milliner's table like banners caught in stillness. There was music, of a kind—a fiddler near the posthouse, bowing a wistful reel, his notes wandering up the chimneys and out to sea. Gulls wheeled overhead, their cries mingling with the calls of vendors hawking fish, bread, pears polished to a shine. I wandered between the stalls accompanied by my new found companion, Una.

"This way, miss," she urged gently, gesturing toward the fruit stall. I obeyed, though my mind was elsewhere.

The fruit gleamed in the morning light—cherries red as spilled wine, plums dark and heavy with sweetness. I reached for one, and in the curve of its skin came a flash of agony; the stair at Marrowhall, white as bone.

The glint of silver in a locked hand.

The silent women writhing beneath their painted masks.

My fingers froze. The weight of memory stole my breath.

"Miss?" Una's voice seemed far away.

The stallholder frowned, reaching to steady the basket as it tilted in my arms. The noise of the street swelled until it pressed against my ears, suffocating.

I stumbled back, colliding with a stranger's shoulder.

The clatter of hooves broke through—carriage wheels swept round the corner, so close it almost blurred.

A cry left my lips as I lurched aside, the hem of my gown brushing the iron rim. The driver cursed, the whip cracked, and the carriage thundered past. I stood rooted, chest heaving, while the market crowd surged on as though nothing had happened. Only Una's hand, firm upon my elbow, steadied me.

"Come, miss," she murmured, her tone brisk but not unkind. "Best return to the house."

❖

Later, in the hush of evening, I sat within my room while Una glided in my surroundings—folding the coverlet back, replenishing my water jug, smoothing the creases in my gown where it had been laid out for the morning. The fire burned low in the grate, and the candlelight drew long shadows up the burgundy walls. The scent of Vanilla hung faintly in the air, mingled with the softness of clean linen and old wood.

Una reached for the brush upon the vanity, but before she could lift it, Lady Hawthorn appeared in the doorway.

"Thank you, Una, you are dismissed." Her voice was not unkind, but it allowed no discussion. Una gave a silent nod and quickly withdrew, the door clicking shut behind her. She traversed across the room with the calm precision of someone used to taking charge in quiet ways, lifted the silver brush and planted her feet behind me. Before her lay my loose hair, falling freely over my shoulders. She began to draw the brush through it—slowly, methodically.

Each soft bristle taming a stubborn knot.

Each stroke smoothing a worry away.

The fire in the grate crackled softly behind us, throwing a warm glow across the rugs, the walls, the folds of Lady Hawthorn's attire. The air smelled of chamomile and old wood. She hummed under her breath—a tune without name or joy, something drifting low, as if dredged up from a memory neither of us could see.

In the mirror, I caught her reflection beside mine. Not as an intruder, but as a silhouette that had always been there. Our profiles near-matched, our brows similarly drawn, though hers were wearied by time and silence. She did not meet my gaze in the glass.

"You must forget the cliff," she said, as though it were an instruction, repeated to herself for years. Her tone was composed. Measured. But there was something beneath it—a hairline crack in the steel.

I said nothing at first. The brush continued its rhythm. Smoothing one more knot. My hands lay folded in my lap, too still.

"And if I cannot?" I asked, not softly but carefully.

Her hand stilled.

Another knot.

The silence that followed felt longer than it was. When she spoke again, her voice was changed. Not broken—but quiet, as though she'd stepped through some door within herself to say it.

"Then you will end up like me."

The fire snapped sharply behind us, sending sparks across the hearth like stars losing their footing. She set the brush down carefully, as if it were a lifeline, then rested her hands atop my shoulders, the weight of them light but steady.

Her fingers smoothed my hair with a touch that startled

me—not because it was rough, but because it was tender. Like casting a spell—no—a blessing perhaps. I could not remember a time that my mother held me with such gentleness. Not held as a ward, not as a creature to be dressed or hidden—but as a daughter, loved for her flaws.

I wanted to ask what she meant. But I did not. I only watched the mirror, and wondered what it had cost her to keep this house, this name, this life built on forgetting.

"There," she said softly, though her tone carried its usual command. "Better."

I could not answer. Grief pressed too near the surface. I had been given safety, a roof, even affection of a kind—but not the affection I longed for. Not the life that had been torn from me by sea and shadow and Marrowhall's hidden rooms. My eyes in the mirror blurred. I blinked, but what rose before me was not the chamber, nor Lady Hawthorne's steady hands, but Marrowhall itself. It drew me still, like the tide.

That night, lying beneath sheets scented with lavender, I could not close my eyes without seeing them—the painted masks, the women's hollow faces, the ring gleaming on that hand. I turned restlessly, my heart beating like a drum.

Closure.

The word came to me unbidden, and with it a terrible certainty. I could not remain here, pretending at peace. So long as Marrowhall stood and my sisters lived in ignorance, I was bound to it. I must return.

Chapter Six

I had never been a woman of the looking glass. Back home, our mirror was a thin sliver, warped with age and cracked at one corner, and I had passed it only long enough to tidy my hair, to check that my gown sat straight, to make certain I would not shame my sisters with untidiness. My reflection had been something to avoid, not to linger upon. But now, in the soft morning light of my chamber, I paused before the glass longer than I ever had. Something in me was altered, though I could not say when or how the change had taken root. Perhaps it was in the set of my shoulders, straighter now, or in the curve of my hips, fuller in their carriage as though the sea had reshaped me when it cast me back.

Upon the dressing table lay a bowl of cherries, the remnant of the morning's market. Their skins gleamed red as blood, as fire, as shame. Without thinking, I plucked one, crushed it between my fingers, and touched the stain to my lips. Another followed, pressed high upon my cheek, leaving a flush that might pass for nature's own.

I startled once more at my reflection, startled at the woman who gazed back. Her lips were red, her cheeks alight, her eyes bright with something perilous, something that had not been there before. Not Tabitha. Not the child who had fled her father's silent halls and her mother's silences. Not the girl who had stumbled weeping into the sea. Alexandra. The name Lady Hawthorne had given me felt alive upon my tongue, a mask that was no longer only disguise but armour. And yet, it frightened me, too. For if Alexandra grew stronger, where had Tabitha gone?

A rap at the door unsettled me. Lady Hawthorne entered, composed as ever, her hair coiled high, her eyes flicking over me with that sharp, measuring gaze.

"You are ready," she said, though I had not spoken a word. I hesitated, clutching the edge of the table.

"I agreed, only to view Marrowhall's gallery with you. The paintings, for inspiration—nothing more." Her voice wavered, when I longed for it to sound certain. I knew well that Lady Hawthorne would never permit my return if she suspected my true intent; that I sought not art, but answers. Concealment, then, was my only weapon — and her company, my only shield.

"If I go alone, I will be noticed. But with you by my side..."

"You will pass unnoticed." Her tone brooked no argument. She sighed, stepped closer, fastening the clasp of a necklace at my throat, its weight cool against my skin.

"Do not forget, Alexandra," she said, her tone low but edged with steel." "You are my guest. You may enter Marrowhall under my guise. You may look, yes — but you must only look. Promise me that is all you will do. I cannot protect you if you falter."

I nodded, though my heart rattled like a bird against its cage. Behind my eyes, I saw again the staircase, the shadows, the painted masks, the hand with its wolf-marked ring. The cherries on my lips tasted suddenly of iron. Yet I lifted my chin, because to return was the only way to silence the sea that still roared in my chest. Closure. The word pulsed again, steady as a drumbeat. And so, when the carriage came to bear us to Marrowhall, I stepped forward and did not look back.

❖

The wheels rattled beneath us as the carriage climbed the coastal road, its pace measured, steady as a heartbeat. Lady Hawthorne sat opposite me, her gaze fixed upon some point beyond the glass, her expression unreadable as always. I, meanwhile, could not keep my eyes from the sea. The cliffs fell sharply away at our right, jagged teeth biting into the waves. I pressed closer to the window, my breath misting the glass, and there—there was the very place. The rocks where I had leapt, the waters that had swallowed me whole.

The sea was restless that morning, white foam rearing high, each wave galloping toward the shore like wild horses with manes of spray. They rose, they crashed, conquered, only to rise again. I shivered, not from cold but from memory. My body remembered the weight of the tide, the choking pull of salt, the thunder in my ears. I pressed a hand against my chest, willing my heartbeat to slow. The water had spared me once. It would not spare me again.

"Keep your eyes ahead," Lady Hawthorne murmured, her voice as sharp as the crack of a whip. I obeyed, though my gaze lingered one moment longer on the restless horizon.

All of a sudden, Marrowhall rose before us. From a distance, it looked unchanged—marble walls, cream stone warmed by the sun, windows glinting like watchful eyes. But as we drew nearer, I saw the difference. The sunlight had tilted westward, so that the shadow of the house fell long upon the earth. That shadow seemed taller than the house itself, stretching over the grounds as though Marrowhall sought to claim more land than stone alone could cover. The gardens lay in fastidious order. Bushes trimmed into precise cones and spheres; gravel walks raked into flawless symmetry. Roses climbed trellises, their blooms scarlet against white lattice, and fountains leapt crystal clear into basins of marble.

On the surface, perfection; yet beneath the hedges, at the roots of the fountains, rot lingered. Brown leaves clung stubbornly to the gravel, swept half-heartedly aside but never fully removed. Moss spread green and damp at the base of carved urns. A single rose hung headless, its petals scattered on the path, already blackening at the edges.

I drew in my breath, for the house seemed to me not only grand but watchful, its windows alive, its walls breathing. A place that was not merely stone and mortar, but something older, hungrier—ready to devour me once more.

The carriage slowed upon the gravel sweep of the drive. The horses tossed their heads, uneasy, their breath steaming. Lady Hawthorne shifted forward; her hands calm upon her lap.

"Remember," she said, her eyes catching mine. "We are here for the gallery. Nothing more."

I swallowed, though the cherries I had pressed to my lips that morning seemed still to stain me, red and raw. As the carriage halted and the footman moved to open the door, I told myself the same. The gallery. Nothing more.

And yet, as I stepped down, the shadow of Marrowhall stretched toward me, and I could not shake the thought that the house had been waiting all this time for me to return.

Chapter Seven

The great doors of Marrowhall opened not onto silence, but a soft hum of life. A crowd pressed within the grand hall, voices murmuring, footsteps echoing across polished marble. Ladies in silks of every hue fanned themselves, gentlemen in tailored coats conversed in polite tones, and children darted beneath skirts before being sharply recalled. Had I not known better, had I not glimpsed what lay beneath this house, I might have thought myself entering a place of peace. There was something of a church to it.

Lady Hawthorne's arm was firm through mine, steadying me against my own pulse. She nodded to this person, inclined her head to that one, greeting them as though she had known each since birth. In return, they looked at her warmly, yet their eyes lingered upon me, puzzled.

"And who is this?" asked a ruddy-cheeked gentleman with a silver-topped cane. Without missing a beat, Lady Hawthorne smiled.

"My goddaughter, Miss Alexandra Greystone. Newly come from Wales."

I managed the small smile she had trained into me, dipping my head in the barest of courtesies. The gentleman seemed satisfied, offered a polite bow, and was swept away in the tide of guests.

"Perfect," Lady Hawthorne whispered, her lips barely moving.

She steered me through the crowd with purpose, pausing before each painting that lined the walls.

"Note the brushwork," she instructed, pointing with her fan.

"See how the artist captures the light? Divine, don't you agree?"

"Yes, Lady Hawthorne," I muttered.

"You must look properly, Alexandra."

"I *am* looking," I replied, though my eyes rolled heavenward. She caught the gesture and gave the faintest laugh, quick and sly, before moving us on. To any passer-by we might have seemed an ordinary pair: a patroness guiding her young companion through a gallery. And for a moment, with the warmth of bodies pressing around us, the lilting music of conversation, I almost believed it myself.

But the memory of her warning returned, sharp as a nail in the carriage's velvet seat.

"You will stay with me at all times," she had said, her gloved hand gripping mine. "He will be here."

"Who?" I had asked.

"Mr Stockholm."

The name alone had sent a chill up my spine, as though it carried with it the weight of chains, the stench of locked doors. I had imagined him already: the master of Marrowhall, the devil in its walls, the one who would have me silenced forever if he knew I lived.

Lady Hawthorne's voice filled my ear again, pointing out another painting, her words like the steady patter of rain. But they faded, dimmed, until they became only a murmur, for something else had seized me. At the bend of the stairwell, half-hidden in shadow, hung a painting.

Horses and carriages, painted in violent strokes, tumbling headlong into the sea. The waves opened to swallow them, the same waves I had once fought. I stepped toward it as though drawn by unseen strings. The rest of the room blurred, voices muffled, Lady Hawthorne's chatter dissolving into silence.

A moth to a flame. A bird leaping from a cliff, wings unformed. I could not look away.

I had climbed halfway up the marble stairwell, its curve sweeping around me like the embrace of some pale serpent, my gaze still caught on that painting. It was vast, gilded, and terrible. Waves rose up like claws, the passengers' faces twisted in frozen terror.

"*Unforgiving*, isn't it?"

The voice came from behind my shoulder — low, deep, with a timbre that seemed to hum through my bones. I startled so violently that my gloved hand flew to the banister, heart hammering in my chest. I turned. The man stood a few steps below, the light of the chandelier catching on the sheen of his dark hair. It fell just long enough to brush his collar, ink-black against the stark white of his cravat. His eyes — God, help me — his eyes were darker still, a fathomless shade did not produce light but in fact absorbed it, held it captive. He was tall. Broader than any man I had ever seen at home. His features might have been carved from obsidian: strong jaw, high cheekbones, a face hardly cut and strangely soft at once, like marble warmed with candlelight.

His suit was severe — black cutaway coat, dark waistcoat with the faintest sheen of silver thread — yet somehow the austerity only sharpened him further.

"You favour it?" he asked, inclining his head toward the painting. His words poured like honey, unhurried, deliberate, designed to be tasted as much as heard. There was no lilt of idle chatter, only an intent that made the air between us taut. I swallowed; my mouth gone dry.

"I... I cannot decide," I admitted, hating the tremor in my voice. "It is dreadful. Yet I cannot look away."

Something flickered across his face — the ghost of a smile, too fleeting to soften him.

"Then the artist has succeeded."

And just like that, he turned, as if the conversation had been nothing. Yet I stood frozen, fingers still curled white against the banister, my pulse loud in my ears.

In that moment, framed by the sea and stair and shadow, I knew that man was unforgettable.

❖

The gallery buzzed around me, as I still stood on the stairwell; polite conversation rising and falling like the tide. Laughter spilled from one corner, the clink of porcelain from another, the rustle of silks brushing against marble floors.

A jolt struck my shoulder. I stumbled, almost falling down a step, breath catching. A gentleman's hand above reached out to steady me.

"Forgive me," he said at once, his brow furrowed as he looked me over. "Did I hurt you? You seemed quite—startled."

I forced a brittle smile, though my pulse still hammered.

"Yes—so sorry—I am quite fine."

"Quite fine," he echoed doubtfully, but I had already drawn back, gathering my skirts. And then, almost against my will, I glanced back down the stairwell.

He was gone.

The man with no name, who had spoken over my shoulder as though he had known me all my life, who had looked at me with eyes so fathomless I feared I might fall into them. Vanished, as though swallowed whole by the shadows.

Lady Hawthorne appeared at my side like a hawk swooping to her perch. Her arm slipped into mine; her smile perfectly polished for the gathering as she swept me forward.

"Come, Alexandra. There is more to see." I let her guide me, though my head turned, desperate, scanning the crowd. My sisters; surely they would still be here—searching, calling for me. Could they not sense I lived? That I had been spared? And then I saw it.

Not them.

The wolf. Etched in black iron above a doorframe, its muzzle raised in a silent snarl. The crest glinted like a wound in the light, and in an instant the flashback seized me—the cold grasp at my skirt, the masked figure, the dancers swaying in time to music I had not heard. The weight of a hand. The glint of a ring. I froze.

Lady Hawthorne's fingers tightened sharply on mine. Her smile never faltered for the crowd, but her words pressed low and fierce at my ear. "Whatever you think you seek, you must not. Alexandra."

The words cut, and yet they steadied me, as though she had pressed a seal over a wound that bled too freely. She leaned in and kissed my forehead, motherly yet commanding, before steering me toward another painting—a pastoral landscape, its serenity a mockery of my unrest. I forced myself to look. To breathe. But from the corner of my eye, across the crowd, I caught him.

The man with no name.

No words passed between us, but my body betrayed me, stilling as though I had been struck. Our gazes caught—his unreadable, mine burning. It was a moment of pure current, a wire drawn tight between two poles.

"Alexandra, Come." Lady Hawthorne hissed; her lips still curved in an elegant smile. Her fingers dug into my arm. "He's here."

The words jolted through me like lightning. Panic clamped its hand around my throat. I could scarcely breathe. Where was he?

"Now," she urged.

Before I could think, Lady Hawthorne had swept me toward the door, our steps urgent yet practiced, her poise never cracking. The crowd swallowed behind us. The air shifted from perfumed marble to the cooler, sobering scent of stone and earth as we hurried outside. A waiting carriage. The slam of its door. The whip of reins. Only then, when the road unwound beneath us, did I realize I was trembling.

Closure? I pressed my palm against my lips, tasting cherries still. No—this was no closure. Pandora's box had been opened.

Chapter Eight

On our arrival back to Penryn House, the sun was beginning to droop behind the sycamores, casting long gold stripes across the cobbles as I wandered through the rear courtyard. I was humming—though I did not realise it at first—a tune half-formed, rising from somewhere deep in the memory of the day. The image of his eyes—the man with no name—lingered in my mind, dark and steady. How ridiculous, I thought, to still feel them watching me here, in this soundless, domestic space.

Then came the crash—

A sharp, splintering sound like a plate flung in rage. It startled a bird from the courtyard roof, and the spinning flower slipped from my fingers.

I turned. The pantry door had burst open, and from it spilled flour—thick white clouds catching the air like smoke. Shards of broken glass glittered in the sunlight. Amidst it all knelt a young girl, weeping quietly, her hands clumsy and red where they'd tried to gather what could not be gathered. She rubbed furiously at her face, smearing flour across her cheeks and lashes. Her dress was far too thin for the late summer season, the hem torn and muddied, the sleeves pushed to the elbow where she'd clearly been scrubbing something far more stubborn than bread tins. A broom lay discarded beside her, and a large sack of flour—now tilted sadly against the stone wall.

I stepped forward. She jolted when she saw me, her hands flying to her apron, though it was already soiled.

"Sorry, miss, I'm sorry—I'll get it cleaned up, swear on my mam's name—the jug slipped, I didn't—"

"It's all right," I said gently, crouching beside her. "You're not hurt?"

She blinked at me, surprised, her breath still hiccupping in her chest. She was a slight thing — narrow of shoulder and pale as morning milk, with wrists too thin for the work expected of them. Her face, though smudged with flour and shadowed by exhaustion, bore the softness of one not yet hardened by the world. A light dusting of freckles marked her cheeks, and her eyes — wide, ocean blue, and terribly earnest — had the look of someone still expecting kindness from the world, though it had rarely shown her any.

Her lips were small, almost petal-shaped, and her nose the tiniest upturn at the tip — the sort of detail a doll might have, if a child had carved her from memory. She had the look of a girl recently plucked from the edge of girlhood, still trailing the fragrance of childhood behind her, though the world had already set to scrubbing it away.

There was beauty there, yes — but not the kind to catch a boy's eye across a room. It was the quiet, enduring sort, the kind that would go unnoticed, only to haunt a boy later.

She shook her head. "No, miss. Just a fright, that's all. Cook told me to get the flour—she said she'd skin me if I was late, but I ran fast as I could—I tripped on the—on the brick that sticks out a bit—."

Her words tumbled over each other like stones down a hill. She reached again for the broken glass with bare hands.

"Stop—let me," I said, catching her wrist. "You'll cut yourself."

She stared at my hand holding hers, as though uncertain if such a thing was allowed. It was then I noticed the chain around her neck—a thin bit of metal glinting faintly beneath her collar. A small oval locket rested against her chest, half-hidden by a fold in the fabric. The name etched into it was delicate, archaic even:

'Loretta Wren'.

She caught my gaze upon the locket, and with that her hand moved at once — protective, almost frightened — as she concealed the locket beneath her collar. A flush rose to her cheeks — not from pride, but the quiet, stinging sort— born from being seen too closely.

"Was a gift," she mumbled. "Nothin' fancy. Just something to remember me by."

"From your family?"

She hesitated. Before I could ask more, the rear door opened and Una stepped in; steady, unfussed, though her eyes found the mess at once, and the faintest sigh seemed to pass through her shoulders.

"Oh, Letty," she exhaled, already rolling up her sleeves.

"I dropped it, miss. I didn't mean to."

"No one ever means to," Una replied, not unkindly however, as she knelt and began sweeping the glass into a dustpan. "Miss Greystone, you needn't—thank you, but I can take it from h—."

"It was my idea to help." I cut in.

Una glanced up at me and smiled, a private sort of smile, the kind shared between women who have seen the sharp corners of the world and softened themselves just enough to survive them. I looked back at the girl.

"Loretta Wren, is it?" She nodded slowly.

"Most call me Letty."

"Have you been long at Penryn?"

"Just two weeks, miss. My da's sick—so I took the place when they offered. Said I was strong enough to carry, and I am. Just not jugs—I suppose." She gave a trembling laugh and rubbed her nose with her sleeve. "Said I'd send home what I could."

There was something in the way she stood—shoulders curled inward, as if already apologising for taking up space—that made my heart ache.

"Then you're doing a brave thing," I said.

Letty looked at me like she wasn't sure if I meant it. Then she nodded, quick and grateful. Una touched my arm lightly. "You've had a long morning, miss. Best leave us to this now. You'll be late for luncheon."

I hesitated, watching Letty scoop what little flour remained back into the bag with shaking hands. I had meant to say something more — to mend perhaps, what I could not name — but the moment, like so many others, slipped quietly past me and was gone.

I nodded. "All right. Thank you, Una."

And as I walked away, each step felt heavier than the last; as though the soles of my boots knew better than I that privilege is not freedom unless it is used. And mine, until now, had mostly been worn like a ribbon — decorative, but of no real use to anyone at all.

❖

By the time I left the drawing room that evening, the teapot had long since emptied and the fire had begun its slow surrender to ash. Lady Hawthorne remained seated in her usual chair, her hands folded neatly in her lap, eyes fixed somewhere beyond the flames — not quite asleep, but no longer in need of conversation. There was a stillness to her that unnerved me — not peace, but the kind of quiet one learns only through resignation.

I wished her a soft goodnight, which she acknowledged with the faintest tilt of her head, and I withdrew with my candle in hand, the corridor stretching out before me like a ribbon of dusk.

The corridor was dim, lit only by the faintest glimmer of oil lamps and the sigh of the wind against the glass. My strides made no sound upon the rug, though the old floorboards murmured faintly beneath them — as if the house knew I had come back changed, bound to another soul.

Una had, as I requested, left a fresh pile of rag paper upon my writing desk. The ink pot had been re-filled, and the nib of my pen set neatly atop the blotter, like a lover waiting for a letter never sent. She had even laid a small square of lavender sachet beneath the inkwell — her quiet way of saying *I see you* without words. The fire still burned low in the grate, its light softening the corners of the room into shadows. Beside me, a single candle flickered — not steadily, but with that strange, wavering motion as though it was stirred by a breath in another realm. I watched it for a moment, unable to shake the feeling that it flickered in rhythm with someone else's thoughts.

Perhaps it was a sign — they were thinking of me. I sat down. The pen felt strange in my fingers at first. Not heavy — no, something else. As if it had waited too long to be used for something honest. I dipped it, watched the ink bloom across the paper like night spilling over the edge of the world. I began:

My Dearest Bea, Marianne, Clara and Liddy,

I do not know whether this letter will find its way to you — perhaps it is foolish to write it at all — but I cannot keep these thoughts inside me any longer.

I miss your laughter — your quarrelling too, even that. The mornings feel empty without the scuffle of your boots in the hallway, the way you used to steal ribbons from my drawer and pretend they'd always been yours.

Do you remember the hills? How we would run through the gorse until our stockings tore and our lungs burned with the joy of it? I think of them now, when the stillness presses too close.

There are things I cannot write. Not yet. Things I have seen and felt that I do not understand, and would not wish to burden you with even if I did. But I am trying. Every day, I rise and try. That will have to be enough.

Tell me you think of me. Tell me I am not a stranger to your thoughts.

Yours always — even now, always,

Tabby

I read it twice over, though I could not say what I hoped to find in the re-reading. The candle gave another strange flutter, like the brush of a sleeve passing too near, and for a moment, I closed my eyes. I imagined them with me — the four of them — standing just behind my shoulder, reading the words as I wrote them, their ghosts not tragic but beloved. With slow hands, I folded the page into thirds and slipped it into an envelope. I did not seal it. Instead, I pressed it to my chest and held it there — not as a farewell, but as a wish, a prayer.

Then, I crossed to the grate. The embers were still warm, glowing like watchful eyes. I lowered the envelope to them, touched one corner to the coal. A flame kissed it gently, curling the edge to black.

I laid it softly among the ashes, watching it vanish word by word.

Not destroyed. Released.

Chapter Nine

Autumn and Winter passed as if it had been a dream. The days slowed, then stretched, until the cold dulled into damp earth and pale buds, and those buds unfurled into the brightness of spring. Time moved strangely in Penryn House; it had none of the hurried rhythm of Wales, none of the constant murmuring tide. It was softer here, hushed, as though the walls themselves conspired to shield me.

Lady Hawthorne kept me busy. In the mornings I walked with her along the edge of the forest, where frost still glittered on the grass but the robins sang as if they alone could summon the sun. Some days she put a brush in my hand and made me paint what I saw: the curve of a branch, a scatter of daisies, the fall of light across the library table. Other days she insisted on riding — chuckling when my posture wavered, praising when I sat taller in the saddle.

She was tireless in her efforts, and slowly, I began to laugh again. Not often, not freely, but enough that the sound shocked me. My reflection startled me, too. I caught myself gazing into mirrors for longer than I once dared. My face no longer seemed like a ghost's. My hips had softened, my cheeks held warmth again; and one day, shamefully, playfully, I crushed another cherry to my lips and let it stain me crimson.

"You will turn heads if you keep on doing so," Lady Hawthorne teased, passing behind me. I rolled my eyes, though a secret smile curved my mouth. It was she who planted the thought in me, one morning as she arranged lilacs in a vase.

"You must not waste away your youth. There is life yet to be lived. There are young men, respectable ones, who would be glad of you."

I made no answer. The words fluttered and fell somewhere inside me, unheeded. For if I closed my eyes, I saw only his eyes — dark as the ocean's depths, endless and inescapable. I tried to pretend they had grown faint with the season's turning, but no spring warmth could melt them. They lived in me still, silent, waiting.

❖

Though I did all that was required of me — rose at the proper hour, wrote daily in my ledger, made myself available for walks and needlework when Lady Hawthorne requested company — I still sought out ways to keep my hands useful. Not out of necessity, for no one expected it, but because it soothed something in me. It made me feel nearer to my old life. Nearer to them.

The clatter of spoons in the kitchen, the hiss of the kettle, the low murmur of voices in the scullery — these were the sounds of my sisters. Or echoes of them. Letty, in particular, reminded me of Marianne — all elbows and effort, prone to stumbling, but full of brightness she didn't know how to carry.

One afternoon, I passed the narrow stair that led to the servants' quarters and glimpsed Una in the laundry room, bent over a steaming press. Her sleeves were rolled to the elbow, a damp cloth in one hand, her brow damp with effort. She moved with a kind of effortless precision, her back straight, her chin high — though no one watched her. There was something almost reverent in the way she handled each garment. I lingered longer than I meant to. Then stepped inside.

"May I assist you?" I asked gently.

She flinched, if only slightly, and straightened.

"Miss Greystone — you really shouldn't—"

"But I must," I said, already reaching for a fresh towel. "I find it helps. Please, allow me."

There was a pause — just long enough for the weight of what I'd said to settle between us. Then Una nodded once, slowly. "If you wish."

We worked in silence for a time — she at the press, I folding linen with what little skill I had left from childhood. There was peace in it. The kind of quiet that asks nothing of you, only your presence.

After a while, I asked, "May I ask your full name, Una?"

She hesitated. I thought she might dismiss the question altogether.

"Una Trelawney," she said at last.

The name fell between us like a coin dropped in a still room — soft in sound, yet unmistakable in weight. I knew it, of course. Everyone did. One of Cornwall's oldest and most storied names — bound to land, law, and legend. A lineage of generals and governors, of estates measured in miles, not rooms. The sort of name not often found amongst cinders and steaming linen.

She must have seen the shift in my expression, for she added, with a lightness that rang too polished to be unstudied, "Not many know it. Most never bother to ask."

"And your family?"

"Scattered," she replied, her voice gentler than I'd heard it before. "Some gone. Some still trying. As they do."

The explanation was smooth, too easily dispensed. As though it had been told before, to others, perhaps even to herself. I said nothing more — only nodded, as though her story satisfied. The thought however, lodged itself within me like a thorn beneath fabric. A *Trelawney*, here, pressing linen beside me? It defied every rule I had come to know. Unless, of course, something had gone terribly wrong.

Or terribly right.

Just then, Letty arrived, breathless and pink-cheeked, with her apron half-tied and her cap askew. Una finally breaking the silence—

"There you are," her voice firm but not unkind. "I've been waiting near half an hour for you."

"Sorry, miss," Letty panted. "Cook had me runnin' the baskets again. Said if I didn't get back fast enough, she'd turn me into soup stock."

Una sighed and gestured to the wooden tub beside her. "You can start by scrubbing these collars. Hot water, and *please* don't scald your hands this time."

"Yes, Miss," Letty chirped, dropping to her knees with more enthusiasm than skill. As she worked, Una leaned over her, showing her how to scrub with a steady, circular motion. "You're flinging water all over the floor Letty. Gentle hands — firm, but not frantic." Letty frowned, tongue poking out in concentration.

"Like this?"

"Better," Una murmured, adjusting her grip. "Now keep it even. You're not chasing rats."

I watched them, a small ache blooming in my chest. There was something almost familial in the way Una guided her — stern, yes, but measured, protective. Like an older sister who had grown used to shouldering the storm, but still took care to shield others from it.

The moment was suddenly interrupted by the echo of soft footsteps behind us. We turned to find Lady Hawthorne at the threshold, her brow lifted, her hands clasped lightly before her.

"Miss Greystone," she said, her voice neutral. "I was under the impression you had taken to your reading."

"I had," I replied, smoothing my skirt. "But I found I preferred movement this afternoon."

Her gaze lingered on my hands — damp now with the scent of lavender soap. Something passed across her face then, something not quite disapproval... but not approval either. When she spoke again, her tone had shifted — only slightly, but I heard it.

"Well," she said. "So long as it brings no harm to the linen." She paused, just a moment — her eyes moving between Una, Letty, and myself. "You have no need to prove your usefulness here, Alexandra," she added, quieter, as if an illusory wall had appeared between us and the girls. "No one will reward you for lowering yourself."

She turned toward the hall, inclining her head with expectation. Una and Letty exchanged brief glances.

"Come. You shall accompany me to the piano room. A woman's posture is best refined at the piano, and it has been some time since I have heard you play."

Her tone left little room for refusal. I rose at once, smoothing my skirts, and placed myself by her side.

❖

When we stepped out into the East passage, the door to the garden stood ajar, and the afternoon light came spilling pale and listless across the flagstones. It was there, beneath the threshold, that I saw it — a small brown shape lying half in shadow.

A bird. A sparrow, perhaps.

I paused, the breath catching in my throat. Its feathers dulled, its sides rising and falling in desperate, uneven rhythm. One wing jutted from its body at an impossible angle, and the look in its dark, liquid eyes was one of bewildered pain.

Oh—" The word broke out before I could temper it.

"Poor thing." Lady Hawthorne followed my gaze, then bent slightly, studying the creature with a practiced coolness.

"Broken wing," she said. "It's been starving for days."

"There must be something we can do." I dropped to my knees before it, ignoring the chill of the stone. "If we wrap it, if we keep it warm—"

Lady Hawthorne's voice cut through mine, gentle but absolute. "It will die regardless."

"We must try," I said quickly.

She folded her hands before her. "My dear, sometimes it is crueller to offer help. To nurse what cannot live is to prolong its suffering — and your own. You will get attached."

"That's not cruelty," I said quietly. "That's compassion."

Her eyes softened, though her mouth did not. "You will learn, Alexandra, that compassion often looks like cruelty to those who still believe all pain can be undone."

For a moment neither of us moved. The bird's breathing grew shallow, its head lolling faintly to one side. Lady Hawthorne drew a slow breath.

"Better to leave it be — or end its misery quickly." She turned then, her skirts whispering against the floor, and gestured toward the drawing room door. "Come. The piano awaits. Music will steady your nerves."

I hesitated. My gaze lingered on the tiny form — its chest still fluttering, defiant against the inevitable. Then I rose, numbed from emotion, and followed her inside. Behind us, the door closed with a soft click, sealing the quiet of the house once more.

"Begin," she said.

But I could not. Each note that came was hollow, faltering — every sound an echo of that faint, dying breath outside the door. Lady Hawthorne corrected my posture, her tone smooth as glass.

"You are distracted, child. The trick of grace lies in detachment." Her words lingered like frost upon the air. Though I obeyed her, striking note after note, I knew then with dreadful certainty that I would never master her art —

for I could not learn to play beautifully while the world lay dying at my feet.

❖

That evening, after dinner had been taken and the fire drawn low in the grate, I returned to my chamber. I had eaten little; the sight of food turned the stomach.

The candle flickered softly beside me as I pulled myself an inch closer to my writing desk. It had become a ritual by then — my nightly confession, written not to be read, but to be released. A letter to my sisters, folded like praying palms and given to the fire.

I wrote of Letty's crooked cap, of Una's steady hands, of the strange ache of belonging and not belonging all at once. I wrote of things I could not speak aloud. And when the ink had dried and the envelope was sealed, I held it to my chest— the way one holds a keepsake or a memory— before saying farewell. I watched it curl once and blacken; my name was the last to vanish into an exhale, breathing the words into oblivion.

Chapter Ten

The morning was bright, the air sharp with green, the kind of air that felt as though it had been freshly washed by the night's rain. Lady Hawthorne knew not of me venturing out alone for the first time, but it was much needed today. I needed space to breathe, alone. Dew still clung to the grass, catching on my riding skirts, and the forest smelled of pine, damp bark, and new life.

My mare moved beneath me in a slow, rhythmic trot, each stride steady, her warmth seeping into my legs. I let the reins fall slack, closing my eyes for a moment, trusting her. The world hushed except for the beat of hooves and the occasional trill of a blackbird. It was the sort of morning that made one imagine futures; the impossible ones, delicate as spindled webs. I thought of what Lady Hawthorne had said; you must not waste away your youth.

A better life. A gentler life. Perhaps, even, a life shared. And then, against my will, those eyes rose in my mind again. Darker than night, darker than the sea at its cruellest hour. They burned not with kindness, but with some fierce recognition; as though he had seen into me and claimed me, without word or touch. A shiver ran through me. Was it dread, or longing? I could not tell.

I shook my head, forcing the image away. Such a future could not exist. He was no man for any girlhood dream. Yet the day was soft, and I could not stop myself from wondering — What would it feel like, to have a hand reach for mine? To lean against a shoulder, to trust? To love, without fear?

The mare's pace lulled me deeper into thought, and I let the air fill my lungs, tasting freedom in it.

Then the world shattered. A crash of undergrowth; a blur of muscle and antler — a stag burst from the trees, wild and magnificent, its hooves drumming the earth. The mare shrieked beneath me, rearing, her muscles jerking against my grip. I clung to the pommel, heart leaping into my throat, the fragile dream torn from me in an instant. She flew forward without mercy, thorns and branches claiming my flesh. I desperately tried to regain control of the reigns, when a voice came behind me — as if it were there, waiting all along.

"Easy there," came the voice, smooth, low, with the confidence of a man long at ease in the saddle. I gasped, clutching the pommel, struggling to calm my breath. When I dared to look, I saw him: a gentleman rider, his coat immaculate despite the chase, his hair pale and touched with sunlight. His eyes — blue, sharp, assessing — softened when they met mine.

"You are unhurt?" he asked.

"I—I believe so," I stammered, my heart still racing faster than the horse beneath me. "Thank you, sir. You came—just in time." He smiled faintly, the corners of his mouth lifting with ease.

"I should hope so. It would be poor sport to let a lady fall while I sat idle." He kept his gloves on as he guided my mare gently back to calm. They were fine gloves, pale leather, fitted close. When at last I found my voice, I said,

"May I know to whom I am so indebted?"

"Edmund Rothwell," he answered with a little bow from the saddle. His smile grew, almost amused. "Though I daresay this is not our first introduction."

I frowned, confused. "I beg your pardon?"

"At Marrowhall," he said lightly. "The gallery. I nearly bowled you over, I recall. Surely you remember?"

A faint heat rose in my cheeks. I searched his face, but the memory did not come. Only the press of the crowd, the blur of shadows.

"Forgive me, sir. I — I do not recall."

Something flickered in his eyes — a brief, sharp wound. He disguised it quickly, his smile easy again, but there was a tightness at the edge of it.

"Forgettable, am I? That is a first."

I forced a small laugh, wishing only to soothe the awkwardness. "It was crowded. I was distracted."

His gaze lingered on me, long enough that the air between us felt too close. Then he laughed also, as though the matter were of no consequence.

"Well, perhaps this time I shall prove more memorable."

He offered to escort me back toward Penrhyn, and I did not refuse. It was the polite thing. But in truth, my heart had not stirred. If anything, it sank.

Chapter Eleven

Edmund spoke most of the way back to Penryn House, his voice smooth, trained, carrying easily over the rhythm of the horses' hooves. He spoke not in arrogance, though he carried himself with an ease that suggested he was accustomed to being listened to. He told me of the countryside, of his travels to London and Bath, of acquaintances and business matters that seemed, at least on the surface, of some importance. He hardly paused, and though I answered politely, I could not help but note how he spoke always of himself. Yet he did so with such grace — each word neatly chosen; each anecdote accompanied by a faint smile that I found myself listening despite my better judgement.

When the horses drew to a slower pace, he leaned slightly toward me, lowering his voice as though confiding in me alone.

"There is little of interest in a man's day-to-day, Miss Alexandra, unless he hopes to appear impressive. I trust I do not bore you?"

I inclined my head, shy, polite. "Not at all, sir." Inside, however, a flicker of doubt unsettled me. Was this what Lady Hawthorne meant — a respectable man, one who would provide a safe path, admired by society? I asked myself if this was the sort of gentleman I might one day be expected to marry. The thought pressed heavily, though I could not name why.

When we reached the gates of Penrhyn, Edmund swung gracefully from his saddle and turned at once to help me down. His gloved hand extended toward me, steady, unhurried. I placed my fingers upon his and let him guide me. For a moment I felt the strength in his grasp, the steadiness, the way he looked directly into my eyes as he handed me to the ground.

"You ride well," he said. "Though the forest can be treacherous." I thanked him softly, my gaze falling. His smile lingered even when I looked away.

It was then Lady Hawthorne appeared at the doorway, her expression brightening with unmistakable delight. "Edmund! My dear nephew." Nephew? The word struck me with a small jolt. She embraced him warmly, as though he were more son than sister's child, and her relief seemed almost palpable, as though his presence were an answer to a silent prayer. She looked then at me, and her eyes softened further, a look passing across her face I could not entirely read — hope, perhaps, or expectation. Edmund, however, seemed to carry the exchange with perfect composure.

He spoke easily of returning from business abroad — a trip that had occupied him for some months. I caught the words, but in the corner of my mind, suspicion stirred. Business abroad? And yet I recalled him mentioning the gallery, his shoulder striking mine in the crowd at Marrowhall. I found myself asking aloud, unable to restrain it;

"Forgive me, Edmund, but — how could you have been abroad, when I met you at the gallery some weeks past?" For the first time his composure faltered. Only for a heartbeat, but I saw it: the faint tightening of his jaw, the flicker in his eyes. Then, smoothly, he laughed, the sound light and dismissive.

"Ah — you are quick to notice. I had returned sooner than expected, though I had not yet made it widely known. Matters of work are seldom as straightforward as one would like. I trust you will forgive the confusion." His tone was so assured, so untroubled, that I felt almost foolish for questioning him. Lady Hawthorne, too, glanced toward me with a gentle shake of her head, as though to urge me not to dwell.

❖

Dinner was already laid that evening in the long hall, firelight casting the walls in warm gold. Hawthorne sat at the head, but it was Edmund who seemed to command the space, though with no overt pride this time. His charm now worked more quietly: the way he listened when we spoke, nodding slightly, as though he cherished even the smallest remark. The way his eyes sought mine, again and again, lingering not with boldness but with something softer — an unspoken admiration.

When I spoke, he leaned forward just a little, his hands resting upon the table, his body turned as though no one else existed. His smile would begin faint, as if only for me, then brighten when I caught it. Once, when the candles flickered and I brushed a stray curl behind my ear, his gaze followed the motion with such intensity that warmth rose unbidden to my cheeks.

"You have a thoughtful mind, Miss Alexandra," he said after one exchange, his tone light but steady. "It is rare, I think, to find such conversation so—refreshing."

Lady Hawthorne, observing us with a satisfied gleam, raised her glass.

"Alexandra keeps my house in good spirits. You would do well to learn from her example, Edmund."

He inclined his head, eyes still upon me.

"I should be glad to try."

Through the courses — roasted pheasant, candied pears, delicate pastries — he remained attentive, never pressing, never allowing silence to fall too heavily. And though I remained cautious, polite, reserved, I could not ignore the way his presence filled the room, or the way my heart stirred unexpectedly when his laughter warmed the air.

Later, when I withdrew to my chamber, the memory of his gaze lingered. Alone, I sat before the mirror, the lamplight soft on my face. I replayed his manner, the admiration in his eyes, the gentleness of his smile.

"You are too callous," I whispered to the girl in the glass. Perhaps Edmund Rothwell was not to be dismissed after all. Perhaps, I thought, I would let myself believe in the safety of his gaze.

❖

It was late — well past the hour when even the most restless chambers had surrendered to sleep. I had just signed my name at the bottom of a letter — to Clara, or perhaps to Mother; I can no longer be certain — when I heard it— A soft sound. Deliberate. The creak of a door opening. I stilled, pen poised mid-air, candlelight trembling faintly against the curve of the ink bottle. For a breath, I told myself it was nothing; just the old house settling, as it often did. But the silence that followed was too careful, too measured.

I rose quietly, careful not to disturb the chair, and took up the candle from my desk. Its flame leaned sideways, as though it, too, were listening. I crossed to the door, turned the handle with practised care, and opened it just an inch.

The corridor beyond lay in velvet shadow, the sconces long extinguished. I stepped into the hush, moving like a breath down the passage, slippers whispering over the rug, until I reached the top of the stairwell.

There I paused—leaning ever so slightly over the banister, concealed by the angle of the wall. Below, the entryway glimmered faintly with lamplight. And within it stood a shadow that did not belong to the night — nor to any hour a girl so young should have known.

Letty.

She did not see me. Placed before the mirror — the one just above the wainscot by the door; her small figure reflected in flickering glass. The chandelier hung above her like pieces of dangling strings. Below, she held a closed tin—turned it over once, then again. It took me a moment to recognise it. Then a flash of crimson caught the light.

It was lipstick. She smeared it across — too wide, too uncertain — then wiped it away with the upper side of her hand. A second attempt; this time thinner, though no more graceful. The red lay heavy on her mouth, ill-fitted and bold — like a dress too large in the shoulders, or a glove stitched with one finger too many. It sat upon her like womanhood itself: borrowed, premature, and bound to slip or smudge. Yet still she pressed her lips together with trembling resolve, as though the ritual alone might summon the woman she believed she ought to be. The effect was truly jarring. Not only from seeing the colour — but because it did not belong. Not on her. Not yet. Perhaps never.

A vase of flowers stood on the console table beside her, now wilted — plucked too early. The scent of them lingered — faintly sweet, but soured now by rot. Something in me twisted. She was trying, in her childlike way, to become someone the world might desire. But this world does not desire—it devours.

Her hair was loose — unbound, gleaming copper in the lamplight. She looked so proud and so fragile, like a moth mistaking candlelight for sunrise. She then adjusted her cap, smoothed her apron, and after one final glance at her reflection, she slipped through the door and vanished into the night. But just before the door closed behind her, the lamplight casted a long, abnormal shape upon the flagstone floor. It was no girl — but a shadow belonging to something narrow and bowed; a bird with its wings pressed close, as though it had never learned to fly.

I did not move. Not for some time. Behind me, the candle fluttered. And down the corridor on my desk, the letter I had written waited — the ink now dry, the words already losing their urgency. I could not return to it. My mind had stilled too deeply.

I returned to my chamber, but sleep did not come that night.

Chapter Twelve

Edmund Rothwell had a gift for presence: wherever he was, the space about him seemed lighter, steadier. It was impossible not to feel it. The next morning, we walked together through the cobbled lanes of the village. The air was fragrant with fresh bread from the baker's door, and smoke curled from cottage chimneys. Children darted about, chasing wooden hoops and tossing sticks into the air, their laughter threading through the clatter of carts. The cheer of it took me back — it was too light for the weight I still carried from the night before.

Before the thought took hold further—Edmund stooped, catching up a small boy who had barrelled into his leg. He lifted him with a laugh, spinning him until the child squealed, the sound bubbling like pure delight. The other children crowded near, tugging at his coat and sleeves, until Edmund, without a trace of hesitation, knelt to their height. He played their game as if he had all the time in the world, his laughter mingling with theirs.

Though sleep had not touched me, I stood transfixed, undone by the quiet peculiarity of the scene. His coat brushed with dust, his gloves smudged with childish fingers — and yet, not once did impatience cross his face. He looked, instead, entirely at home. When at last he returned to my side, I felt the warmth of his nearness with more keenness than I wished to admit. He brushed the air from his sleeve with a wry smile, then turned his gaze on me. Something softened there, as though he saw not the street nor its bustle but only me.

"You've an eyelash," he murmured. His gloved hand rose with surprising gentleness, brushing just beneath my eye. The cold touch lingered no longer than a breath, yet the world seemed to still around it. I caught myself inhaling, my cheeks warmed, my heart oddly unsettled.

We continued, arm brushing arm, until the market square opened before us. Stalls spilled with apples, flowers, trinkets of polished brass. At the flower stall, he paused. Without ceremony, he plucked a small bloom; white, with a heart of gold. He pressed a coin into the vendor's palm. Turning to me, he offered it with a little bow, a boyish smile curving his lips.

"For you, Alexandra. A poor gift perhaps, but it suits you."

I took it, unable to stop the warmth that rose in my cheeks. "You are kind," I murmured, tucking the flower carefully into the ribbon at my wrist.

Yet as we moved further down the street, the air shifted. Houses stood half-crumbled, their windows boarded, their gardens gone to briar. A child sat barefoot on a doorstep, knees drawn to her chest; a man leaned against a wall, cap in hand, his eyes hollow. The faint scrape of a beggar's bowl followed us as we passed, tin against stone. Edmund's smile thinned.

"The mines," he said, with a sharpness that suggested a subject too often spoken of. "Tin, copper." He raised his chin, "Once, every man here had work enough to fill his belly." He gestured lightly, almost impatiently, toward the ruin about us. "Now the workers drift. Some emigrate.

Others beg. And others..." He let the word linger, heavy, as a man crossed the street with a furtive glance, "turn to less savoury trades. Desperation is fertile ground for corruption."

I said nothing at first, only gripped the flower in my hand until its stem bent beneath my glove. For I had seen hardship before— back home— during the long winters, families pressed close in cottages where slate dust settled into every seam, where bread was stretched thin and children grew pale. I only heard of long hours for low wages that left mountains hushed — men passing with lung disease, women with hands raw from washing for neighbours, just to keep a candle burning.

Yet this was different. This was ruin made visible: whole houses gutted, streets choked with silence, hunger etched into each face. I had thought, once, that my family struggled. But we had always been shielded by the illusion of dignity, our poverty softened by pride and by the walls that kept the world out. Here there was no veil. The collapse of these mines had stripped everything bare.

It struck me then with a force I could scarcely admit — how much I, as Tabitha, had been sheltered. How ignorance had once bound me in ribbons and lace, kept me from seeing how the world gnawed at those who had nothing left to give. And now, standing at Edmund's side, I could feel that world of innocence thinning evermore, exposing corruption, to the dark truth of survival— at any cost. Edmund's voice broke into my thoughts, softened now, almost confiding.

"It is the way of this country: when one door closes, another opens. Not always a virtuous one." He did not name Marrowhall, let alone the hidden rooms, or Letty smearing the lipstick, but something spoke to me as if there was connection between them.

Soon after, we left the press of the streets behind and rode out along the forest path. The afternoon sun dappled the ground as we rode side by side, the woodland unfolded to either side of us in a canopy— an embrace of green. The air smelled of pine and fresh rain, the mare's hooves drumming a steady rhythm upon the softened earth.

I kept my mount to a steady pace, the reins loose in my hands, but my thoughts lagged behind—in the alleys, in the hollow faces, all the way to the back of my mind—to Letty.

"There is so much suffering," I said, more to the wind than to Edmund. "Hunger that clings like a second skin. And we walk off, ride on, as if not seeing were a virtue." I hesitated. Even when it knocks at our own door, wearing red on its lips.

"It does not sit well with me. I cannot help but wonder what might be done—could be done, even."

Beside me, Edmund shifted in the saddle. His voice, when it came, was soft—soothing, even.

"You mustn't trouble yourself with such things, Alexandra." He smiled at me, the kind of smile one might offer a child who's asked why the sky turns dark.

"It is a man's duty to shoulder the burdens of the world. These matters—poverty, reform, policy—they belong in Parliament, in ledgers, in the hands of those trained to manage them." He spoke kindly, with the confidence of one who had never questioned the order of things.

"The world has its ways, Alexandra. And for the most part, it does function."

He didn't sound unkind. Just—certain. As though the matter had long been decided by minds greater than mine. A part of me wanted to argue. But what would I say? That I had glimpsed sorrow in the market, in the very walls of my own home, and felt moved to action? I had never held office, never written policy, never experienced true plight myself to ever comprehend. What did I know of solutions? Perhaps he was right. Perhaps it was arrogance to believe I might change anything. Still, there was something in the way he spoke—something that didn't quite belong to him. As if the words had been placed seamlessly in his mouth long ago, and he'd never thought to question their shape.

I looked at him then—not for the first time, but truly looked—and saw not cruelty in his reasoning, but something perhaps—even colder: comfort, wrapped in manners. A man not wicked, but one who had never been asked to pay the cost of his comfort. I turned my face back to the road. The wind picked up, sharp against my cheek, and I said nothing more.

Edmund, however, would not allow silence to linger. He spoke freely, the cadence of his voice carrying us along the road. I listened politely, answering when courtesy demanded, but more often letting his words wash over me and my troubled thoughts, like the hum of a tide. Still, there were more moments when he disarmed me — the way he looked at me not as though I were a companion to entertain, but as though I were the subject of his admiration—when his hand guided my reins across a rough patch of ground, when his laugh initiated a break of light in the clouds to open.

I wondered—could this be the man society might expect me to favour? He was respectable, charming, attentive. Surely no one would question it. And yet, deep within me, the shadow of darker eyes stirred.

We eventually crested a bend in the road, the view opening out toward the rolling fields beyond. That was when the rhythm broke. Another rider approached.

His horse was taller, broader, black as pitch; its stride a controlled power that drew the eye. The man upon it wore a dark coat, his gloved hand steady upon the reins. His top hat cast his face half in shadow, though the clean line of his jaw and the cut of his frame spoke of strength contained. As he neared, even my mare shivered beneath me, sensing perhaps what I had not yet put into words. Edmund straightened in the saddle, his voice carrying easily across the narrowing space.

"Stockholm."

The name fell like iron into the air.

The rider drew his horse to a halt, and for the first time his face was revealed. His gaze flicked toward me only briefly, as if my presence was of no consequence — and yet that glance seared me, so sharp and unblinking it seemed to brand itself upon my skin. My blood ran cold.

I knew those eyes.

"Rothwell." His voice was smooth, deliberate, carrying authority without effort. Their exchange one of acquaintanceship—ordinary, almost cordial. Yet from my seat, I felt the world contract, the space between them taut as wire. I sat frozen, my heart pounding beneath my ribs.

The two conversed with ease, but my thoughts clattered too loudly to make sense of what was said. I watched instead — not his words, but the cut of his coat, the quiet assurance in the way he stood, the precise tilt of his head as he listened to Edmund.

I knew him.

Not by name—no, not then—but by something older. Older than breath. Older than sense. He was the man from the gallery, the stranger who had watched me like I was not simply seen, but remembered from a past life. The one whose gaze had followed me from canvas to corridor. The one whose presence had lived beneath my very skin ever since. But more than that — *he* was Stockholm.

The name alone tore through me like a cry in a locked room. I had carried it like a wound stitched too tightly, belonging to the man in the shadows, the myth tied to my ending — to hers. To Tabitha. Now standing before me, so still, so real, so dreadfully unchanged from the day at the gallery. My breath caught, though I did not falter. My hands remained folded, my expression calm. But somewhere within me, the floor had given way. I felt myself spiralling, soundless, like a bell dropped down a well — rung, but never heard.

I straightened, though it took every ounce of strength I possessed. To falter now would be foolish — a perilous crack in the mask I had so carefully worn. Fear, if shown, would be read like a map. And this man, this man was dangerous. Yet each breath seemed harder won than the last— shallow, strained, as though the very air had turned against me. My chest tightened; the air pressed in. Yet still I dared not look away.

His eyes, what if they found mine—properly this time? What if he recognises me? Not as I sat now, draped in composure and silk, but as I once was — as she was? I drew my netted veil lower with trembling fingers, turning my face as if to shield against the sun. But before I could fill my lungs with another breath, fear betrayed me, and I slammed my heel to the mare's side. She leapt forward, startled into motion.

I sliced between the two souls like lightning splitting through an oak tree. The forest blurred past as I hurtled down the road, breath ragged, cloak whipping behind me. My heart beat with a single word.

Run.

❖

Hooves thundered beneath me, wild and desperate, as though the mare herself carried my fear in her chest. Branches tore at my sleeves, brambles lashed my skirts, and still I urged her onward, heedless of the scratches and the sting of air in my lungs.

The path narrowed. Blinded by fear, I did not see it until it was too late—the forest broke, and before me stretched a sheer cliff, the sea raging below. The mare reared, and I yanked the reins whilst my body nearly pitched forward into the abyss. Pebbles skittered over the edge, vanishing into white spray and the roar of waves. For a moment, everything stilled. My heart beat louder than the ocean crashing below. I pressed my face into the mare's mane, trembling. The salt wind tore at my hair, twisting it about my cheeks like wayward strands of grief — and still the question echoed through me, fierce and unrelenting: How could I have been so senseless?

I saw his eyes once more — rising from the sea-mist, dark and merciless, unyielding as the tide. Had I mistaken them? Mistaken desire for safety, curiosity for care? Had my own heart turned faulty, so wholly that I could no longer tell shadow from light? Shame struck sharper than the cuts upon my skin. What folly it was — to seek tenderness where there was none, to imagine gentleness in a gaze I could not even name. To dream of safety in a man who had offered me nothing but death.

Where had the ring been that day in the gallery? No band glinting a wolf's snarl in the light? Had I imagined it? Or worse — was memory itself now a suspect, a traitor turned against me? I had thought him a spectre of possibility, a figure conjured from some half-forgotten prayer — a promise that youth need not be wasted, nor affection misplaced. And yet there he stood today, not ghost, but man — flesh and form, bearing a name that cleaved me open with a violence I could not withstand.

How blind I had been. How ruinously foolish, to dream — even for the briefest moment — of futures drawn from his gaze. To imagine tenderness where none had even been offered. To believe I might be seen, truly seen, by eyes I had never even earned the right to name.

I pressed my palms against my eyes, hard enough to blur the world. As if I could scour him from me — from memory, from breath, from blood. But still he clung; his eyes, his presence, his unbearable nearness. I turned the mare sharply from the cliff's edge, her hooves tearing into the soft earth as she leapt back into the shrubs.

We plunged back into the woods; branches whipping, the air thick with pine and damp moss. My breath came fast, broken, but I urged her on, faster, farther; as if his spirit was chasing me—hunting me down. I would outrun him if it cost me the last breath I possessed.

When at last the house came into sight—pale against the bruised edge of evening—I slowed her to a canter, then a walk. My body trembled with the effort of keeping upright. My cheeks burned, my throat raw from weeping, yet still the storm inside me did not quiet.

Edmund flickered at the edge of my mind — a quieter presence, a murmur of steadiness. Of gentleness. I felt again the flower at my wrist, pressed there by his hand. And for one fragile moment, I longed to lean into that calm — to be held in it. To be safe. But the thought dissolved before it could settle. Swallowed by the taste of betrayal.

Not now. Not when I had betrayed myself so utterly — by trusting the devil in borrowed light, and letting my heart wander where it had no right to go.

I slid down from the mare before the steps of Penryn, my skirts completely torn, arms streaked with scratches, each stripe likened to lashes of a whip. For a moment I stood there, fists curled tight around the reins, and the weight of it — of all I had seen, all I had believed — pressed down upon me until I feared I might sink into the stone beneath my feet and be lost to it. Turned to granite. Forgotten.

Instead, I pressed my forehead to the mare's neck, the warmth of her breath rising steady beneath my cheek. I whispered into her coat — not words, but fragments, the broken language of sorrow, as though she might bear what I no longer could. And so, I led her through the gates, my fingers still trembling, the dusk folding round us like mourning cloth. The night came fast behind me, and still his name echoed in my chest — unspoken, but burning.

❖

The night had turned heavy, the air thick as damp linen. I could not eat; Una had brought a tray to my chamber — broth, bread, a sliver of apple tart — and I had thanked her softly, but my stomach turned at the sight of it. I wept until my eyes burned and my throat was raw. No letters tonight; my thoughts were too jagged for ink. I blew out the candle and turned from the window, drawing the covers over me as though they might muffle memory itself.

At last, sleep overtook me; yet it came as all mercies do — reluctant, and heavy with unease. How long it held me, I cannot tell; where a sound stirred me — faint, broken — drifted through the corridor beyond my chamber at first, I assumed it was the wind against the glass, but then it came again: a sob, thin and trembling, too human for the hour. I sat upright, heart thudding.

After a moment's hesitation, I reached for the candle at my bedside. Its flame shivered into life, small and uncertain, a single trembling star amid the gloom. The wax had burned low; its scent was faintly sweet, mingled with the chill breath that stole in beneath the door. I slipped from the bed, the floor cold beneath my bare feet, and wrapped my shawl around my shoulders. Its wool was rough against my skin, yet I drew it tighter, as though it might lend courage where I had none.

The latch turned with a sound too loud for such stillness. The door gave a soft sigh as it opened, and a thread of cold air crept inward, licking at the flame until it quivered perilously. The passage was dim, long and narrow, the wainscoting blackened by age. Shadows moved faintly along the walls, drawn by the flicker of my candle — silhouettes that seemed to breathe and bend as I passed. The house had fallen utterly silent, save for the faint ticking of the clock on the landing and, beneath it, the sound that had roused me: a low, uneven sobbing, rising and falling like the sea beyond the cliffs.

I hesitated at the head of the stair. The air was cooler here, touched by the damp of the stone below. The great house slept around me, heavy and unaware. I might have been the only living soul within it — and yet, the sound below told me otherwise.

The crying came again. Muffled. Desperate. It was the cry they whisper about along the cliffs of Boscastle. The cry that comes before the sea *takes*. A warning, or a remembrance; no one ever knows which.

I held the candle close, cupping my palm about its fragile light, and began my descent. Each step groaned faintly beneath my tread. I moved as though through water — slow, weightless, every breath deliberate. The shadows deepened as I neared the landing, and still the weeping continued, drawn-out and hopeless, threading itself through the silence like something half-human, half-haunting.

By the time I reached the curve of the staircase, my heart was hammering so loudly I feared it would give me away. I found the same narrow step where I had once sat before —

the one worn smooth at the edge, a secret perch between shadow and sight. Here I could see without being seen; a quiet sentinel poised between two worlds — the sleeping chambers above and the feverish hush of the household below.

Beneath me, the hall stretched wide and still — a theatre of silence awaiting its performers.

Two figures stood by the dying fire.

Letty — small, trembling, her apron crumpled in her fists — was weeping openly. Her head was buried against Lady Hawthorne's shoulder. it might have seemed an act of tenderness, of compassion from Hawthorne. However, to me the gesture held a curious stillness, as though rehearsed. Her hand moved in slow, mechanical strokes through Letty's hair. It was the same hand that had once passed, slow and deliberate, through my own — soft enough to imitate affection, but empty of its pulse.

Letty's voice broke through the quiet.

"He promised I'd be safe." She whispered.

My breath caught. *He?*

Lady Hawthorne's expression did not alter. "Hush now, child. There is nothing to be gained from tears."

"I—must tell—"

The rest was lost. Lady Hawthorne drew her closer, pressing the girl's face against her shoulder.

"There, there," she murmured. "Compose yourself. You are tired. You will make yourself unwell."

Her tone was tender, but her eyes — those fine, pale eyes — were fixed somewhere beyond the girl's bowed head. Detached. Assessing. It was comfort offered without heat; mercy performed for the sake of witness alone. The fire spat softly. Letty's sobs quieted into small, strangled sounds. I leaned forward, unable to stop myself. My knee brushed the floorboard.

It creaked— Both heads turned sharply upward.

Lady Hawthorne's face lifted toward the stairs — not startled, but searching. The firelight caught her eyes, and for a fleeting instant they gleamed — not with fear, nor protectiveness, but with a cold, lucid hunger to know who had *dared* to listen.

I froze. Then, panic seizing me, I stumbled back, pressing a hand over my mouth. The flame trembled. I turned and fled, the hem of my gown whispering against the steps, straight into my chamber once more. I shut the door and leaned against it, shaking from pure adrenaline. I was a mouse that had darted from a trap., still trembling from the snap of its jaws. The candle suddenly guttered and went out.

Once I regained some control in my legs, I clambered into bed, pulling the coverlet over my head like a child warding off ghosts. But no cloth could muffle the sound that lingered in my ears — Letty's cries, and a burning question. *Who was 'he'?*

The cries went on a while longer — softer, distant, then gone — leaving only the hush of my own pulse.

Sleep eventually took hold of me, though I could not say when. I drifted somewhere between waking and forgetting, where even fear grew quiet. By morning, I could not tell if the tears had been hers — or my own.

Chapter Thirteen

The days that followed passed in uneasy quiet. My arms bore scratches like nettle stings, my body stiff with bruises, yet none of it troubled me so much as the tumult in my chest. I begged Lady Hawthorne to write to Edmund on my behalf, saying I had fallen unwell after what had happened in the forest. It was not wholly a lie — though no fever gripped me, my mind was ill with unrest, my sleep shattered by the echo of hooves and the sound of a name I could not shake.

Edmund's letters came swiftly, anxious in their tone. He fretted that he had spoken amiss, that I had taken offence at some careless remark. The longer I stayed away, the more his words betrayed his unease. He asked if he had done something wrong, if my sudden withdrawal was his fault. I answered only in short, polite notes, assuring him it was not him — never him — but his doubts seemed to grow with each day I kept to Penryn's walls.

Lady Hawthorne, ever perceptive, would not let me retreat into shadow. She set about my recovery with gentle determination, ensuring that I walked the garden paths when the air was mild, that I took broth when my appetite waned, and that I did not let sorrow bend my shoulders. Yet when Edmund's latest letter arrived — an invitation to a gathering that promised cheer, music, and company — it was she who pressed it into my hands and said, firmly, "You must go."

And so, though my heart trembled, the day arrived.

❖

I woke with a start, my heart hammering against my ribs. The room was dim, the light from the window a thin grey mist across the floorboards. I sat up, breath caught, unsure if I had screamed or only dreamt of doing so. A voice — a cry — still rang in my ears.

Letty's cry. For a moment I could see her: the round of her pale face, her eyes wide with tears, her lips moving in desperate whisper. Then the vision dissolved into the folds of sleep, leaving only its echo behind. I pressed a hand to my temple. I had not seen her for days — not since that night—Since that nightmare on the stairwell. Or had I dreamt it at all? Perhaps I had simply been lost in my own misery, so consumed by the revelation of my own attentions I had withdrawn entirely from the life of the house.

The image of Letty's tears returned to me again and again, and each time it came sharper, more real. With sudden dread, I threw back the coverlet and rose. The floor was ice beneath my feet, the air unkind against my skin.

In the looking glass, my reflection was ghostlike — hair unbound, eyes dark with restlessness. A sound in the corridor made me turn. Lady Hawthorne stood at the far end, gloved and immaculate, a riding crop in hand. She looked as though she had already lived an entire morning before I had even begun mine.

"Good morning, Alexandra," she said, her tone light but brisk.

"Good morning—" I tried to match her tone, but failed.

"A smile, my dear, costs nothing."

Her words took me back, yet I obeyed, forcing the corners of my mouth to lift.

"Better," she said. "Edmund will expect to find you radiant this evening. You cannot afford to appear miserable."

She turned, her steps measured as ever, and disappeared into the morning light beyond the hall.

For a long moment I stood motionless, the echo of her words hovering in the air like dust. Could I have imagined it all — Letty's sobbing, Lady Hawthorne's cold embrace? The thought gnawed at me.

I gathered my shawl and made my way down the servants' passage. The scent of soap and damp linen grew stronger with each stride. A low murmur of voices drifted from the laundry room, where steam rose in pale clouds.

Elsie was there, sleeves rolled, her arms red from the heat of the tubs. When she saw me, she startled — not out of disrespect, but wariness.

"Miss," she said quickly, curtseying. "I didn't hear you come in."

"I'm looking for Letty," I said. "I haven't seen her since—since earlier this week."

Elsie's gaze flicked away. Her face had gone curiously pale. "She— she's not here, miss."

"Not here?"

"She must've run off," Elsie replied after a pause. "With her lover, most likely. There'd been talk of it."

I stared at her. "Run off?"

Before she could answer, the cook — a stout, ruddy woman from the adjoining kitchen — leaned round the doorway, wiping her hands on her apron.

"You'll waste your pity, Miss," she said, half-smiling.

"The girl handed in her notice two mornings past. Couldn't handle the work. Scullery maids come and go — they've no stomach for it. Always some sweetheart waiting to whisk them off." Her tone was flippant, almost cheerful. I could only watch her as she returned to her chopping board, humming a careless tune. It made no sense. If Letty had gone willingly, why had she wept so bitterly that night? The thought twisted in me like a thorn.

Footsteps sounded behind us. The gamekeeper and his men had returned from a morning shoot; boots muddied and arms heavy with game bags, feathers peeking from the seams like a silk pillowcase.

The cook laughed — a short, high bark — as one of the footmen dropped the spoils onto the table with a thud. The air filled with the scent of feathers and death.

"Six hens, four woodcocks, and this little thing," he said, holding up a limp bird no larger than a clenched fist. "Barely worth the powder."

The others laughed. The bird was young — a fledgling, by the look of it. Its wings still soft, its eyes sealed in death. Its beak hung open as if mid-song. One of the boys poked at it with a skewer, as though testing for life. It rolled across the wooden surface, graceless, still warm.

I turned away, stomach twisting. Lady Hawthorne entered; her cheeks flushed from the cold. She wore her riding habit, the crop still in hand. Her lips curved faintly at the limp creature.

"A good eye," she exhaled. "Even the smallest marksman's prize deserves praise."

He held the bird higher as a final decree of pride — a pitiful, limp thing, no larger than my hand. The memory of the sparrow beneath the steps flooded back — the frail tremor of its breath, the indifference with which she had walked away. I could not stand another moment longer.

"A new scullery maid arrives tomorrow," Lady Hawthorne casually announced, "Please see to it that she receives proper instruction."

And with that, she walked on — her heels clicking smartly across the stone, her shadow trailing behind her like the hem of a garment too heavy to carry. I stood there a long while, staring at the trail of feathers across the floor — white, soft, and speckled with blood. The baby bird lay forgotten upon the table. The scent of iron clung to the air, sweet and sharp, and I thought of Letty's voice in the dark — that broken sob that might have been the wind. Everyone had turned away, and the house had swallowed her whole. Was this how the world forgot its daughters? With the same careless grace that left a bird to stiffen on a kitchen board?

I wanted to scream, to call her name aloud, to demand for answers — but the words turned to salt in my throat.

❖

Evening pressed soft and golden against the glass, yet the light did nothing to lift the heaviness that had settled over me. Letty's absence hung in the air like smoke — clinging to the edges of thought, impossible to brush away.

I had done little all afternoon but wander the rooms, fingers restless, mind turning endlessly upon itself. Each creak in the corridors made me start; each shadow at the door I hoped might be hers.

When Una entered my chamber, her quiet presence steadied the air; carrying the faint scent of lavender and lemon — the scent of order. She said little — she rarely did — but I had begun to find a kind of comfort in her company, as if the air stilled when she entered. It settled my nerves.

"You'll be late dressing, miss," she said softly, setting a folded gown upon the chair. I turned from the window.

"Una, have you any word of Letty??" The question slipped out before I could contain it. Her hands stilled. For a moment, she did not answer. Then, with careful composure, she said,

"No miss, perhaps she has gone to her kin."

"So abruptly? Without farewell?"

Una hesitated, her eyes flicking to mine — quick, assessing.

"I'll ask in the kitchens," she said at last. "Quietly. Sometimes these things— take time to unfold."

Her tone was calm, but I caught the faint tremor beneath it.

"You think something's happened," I said.

"I think," she replied gently, "that worry seldom helps before we know what is true."

Her answer did not comfort me, yet the steadiness in her gaze did. She was not one to leave a matter unresolved. I knew she would find what she could — and for now, that had to be enough.

I drew a breath. "Thank you, Una."

She inclined her head, her manner brisk again.

"Now — let us have you ready." She crossed to the wardrobe and drew out a gown the colour of soft rose — its fabric fine, the sleeves gathered in pale lace.

"This one, I think," she said, holding it against the light.

I smiled faintly. "You always choose such colours."

"They are kind to you, miss," she said, eyes warm. "There is strength enough in gentleness. You need not armour yourself in darkness."

I might have answered, but before I could, the door opened and Lady Hawthorne entered. Her silhouette cut sharp against the corridor light; her composure unflinching as ever. That was until her gaze met the dress.

"That is far too pale for an evening such as this. You must not fade into the wallpaper, Alexandra. Men respect confidence, not softness. Try the maroon silk — the one with the darker trim. It stands taller." Her gaze lingered upon me — not cruelly, but with that well-meaning weight that feels like a hand pressed too long on the shoulder.

I felt myself suspended between them, then at last, I reached for the gown Lady Hawthorne named.

"The maroon, then," I said.

Her satisfaction was quiet, triumphant in its restraint.

"Good," she murmured. "You'll find the colour compliments your complexion."

The gown chosen was of deep crimson silk, its sheen shifting in the candlelight from scarlet to burgundy, rich as the deepest wine. The bodice fitted close, the skirts fell in sweeping folds, and fine embroidery stitched along the hem glimmered faintly like threads of flame. My hair was dressed into loose ringlets, brushed until they shone, the curls falling against my collarbones in soft spirals. A touch of rouge warmed my cheeks, a faint tint darkened my lips. When at last I dared to look in the glass, I scarcely knew the reflection that gazed back. The pallid girl I had once been was gone. In her place stood a woman burnished by colour, by poise, by the faint suggestion of something unspoken — resilience, perhaps, or the will to begin again. I drew a breath, steadying myself.

Then a sharp rap sounded at the door. A butler's voice followed, clipped and formal.

"He has arrived, madam."

My pulse quickened. Lady Hawthorne's reflection straightened in the glass before I could turn. "So early? Then we mustn't keep him waiting." Her tone was brisk, almost eager — as though the gravest sin a woman could commit was to keep a man waiting.

She swept out of the door, skirts whispering like reprimand. Just before I proceeded to leave the room with her, I sat at my vanity to fasten my earrings. My hands, unsteady with the rush of it all, fumbled at the clasp — the kind of small failure that betrays what one means to conceal. Una, still omnipresent moved silently through the room, apart from the faint rustle of linen and scent of lavender following her as she laid out my shawl. She approached to adjust the collar of my gown, then paused, tilting her head.

"Will Mr. Rothwell be accompanying you tonight?" she asked, eyes fixed on a wayward curl.

"Yes." I said, glancing toward the looking-glass. "Why?"

She said nothing — only smoothed the edge of my sleeve. There was something in her stillness; a flicker of tension, like a thread pulled too tight, with barely a breath's hesitation. Before I could press further, Lady Hawthorne swiftly re-entered.

"Come now, child, there's no virtue in keeping a gentleman waiting." She beckoned, flustered in her motion.

In response to my question, Una gave a small nod and stepped back; as though deciding it was not her place.

"Shall I bring your hair pins, miss?"

"Oh — yes, thank you." I decided to not press further. And that was all.

"Beautiful." Lady Hawthorne said simply, fastening the last pin that Una had swiftly delivered. At my throat she clasped a necklace of garnet drops, the stones catching and holding the light like small, pulsing hearts. They gleamed— delicate, obedient — and for a moment I almost believed the woman staring back might belong to this world of polished hearts and practiced smiles.

The thought sat heavy as I reached for my purse and turned toward the corridor. The silence Una had left behind seemed to follow me however — it was not accusing, merely stirring something restless in me, like a note of music that refused to fade.

Chapter Fourteen

I paused at the top of the stairwell, my gloved hand resting upon the polished banister. Below, the hall shimmered with candlelight — soft gold trembling across marble and gilt. I could hear Lady Hawthorne's voice in greeting, then the low timbre of a man's reply.

Breathe, I told myself. Do not falter.

Gathering my skirts, I began my descent. The silk whispered faintly against the carved oak, each step deliberate, rehearsed, as though composure itself might steady me. At the foot of the stairs stood Edmund Rothwell, his back turned toward me. He was adjusting his cravat, smoothing his coat, brushing some imagined crease from his waistcoat — small, precise motions that spoke of a man preparing to be seen. I had never before witnessed him so intent, so quietly flustered, as though even his posture sought approval.

Then he turned.

For a moment he seemed struck still, the words caught behind parted lips. His gaze swept over me, reverent, disbelieving. The light seemed to leave him, only to return in his eyes.

"Alexandra…" His voice was hushed, almost unsteady. Then, recovering himself, he smiled — not his usual effortless charm, but something warmer, almost hopeful.

"You look sensational."

A warmth rose to my cheeks before I could stop it. I lowered my gaze, one hand resting on the curve of the banister. The smile that came was small, unbidden — and though neither of us spoke again, the air between us said everything. He stepped forward then, extending his hand. The gesture was simple, as if practiced — yet there was a tremor in it, as though he feared I might refuse. For a heartbeat, I hesitated at the final stair, the world narrowing to the space between us.

Then, slowly, I placed my hand in his.

The touch lingered — his fingers closing around mine, steady, warm, possessive. Candlelight shimmered through the crystal pendants above, scattering gold across the marble floor, across his hair, across the crimson silk of my gown.

For one suspended instant, everything stilled — the air, the breath, the pulse. Edmund reached for my shawl and draped it gently across my shoulders, his movements deliberate, unhurried, each one the mark of a true gentleman. He guided me toward the door with quiet grace, opening it to the night and the waiting carriage beyond.

"Shall we?" he said softly.

And with that, I stepped out into the world's embrace.

His eyes did not leave me, not even as he handed me inside with care. I felt the intensity of his admiration as though it were another cloak about my shoulders, heavy and unshakable.

❖

The wheels turned, carrying us through the twilight toward the great house where the gathering awaited — the Hastings family's residence, Hawkstone Manor, if memory serves. And what a spectacular estate it was. Lamps glowed at every window, their golden light spilling across the manicured lawns, trimmed to exactness. Even before we drew to the entrance, I could hear the faint hum of strings and laughter carried upon the air.

Inside, the scene was one of splendour. The ballroom unfolded in a sweep of gilt and crystal: chandeliers dripping with light, their prisms scattering jewels of colour upon polished marble floors; walls draped in silks of ivory and gold; long tables laden with dishes gleaming under silver domes — roasted pheasant, sugared fruits, glazed violets glistening in glass bowls. The air was warm with candle smoke, perfume, and the faint bite of wine.

The guests moved like a river of silk and satin, voices rising and falling in laughter, in the murmurs of gossip and admiration. Glasses chimed as they were lifted, champagne foaming pale and delicate within. Laughter broke into bursts around the card tables, where fortunes were risked with a flick of the wrist, a roll of the dice. In the far corners, smoke curled where gentlemen gathered, cigars in hand, their eyes darting across the room between wagers.

Edmund's hand rested voraciously at my waist as we strode, his fingers splayed just enough to be felt through the fine fabric of my gown. He greeted nearly every guest as we passed, offering the same smile he wore in the village that day — polished, effortless, unreadable. With each polite nod, each murmured "Good evening, Mr Rothwell". It seemed he was the guest, and I — his decoration.

His grip never faltered. Then, his gaze shifted toward the cluster of gentlemen gathered near the hearth — a tight knot of conversation and smoke, cut off from the rest of the room as though they answered to no one but themselves.

"There they are," he murmured close to my ear, the warmth of his breath brushing my cheek. "Come."

Before I could question who, I felt a subtle pressure at my back, and was swept towards them like a leaf caught in a gust of wind, helpless to the tide of his will. The velvet crowd parted before him.

Their conversations were low and well-oiled, the kind that slid between finance and flirtation without ever settling. I hovered just outside the circle, glass now in hand, the music of the evening a distant hum beneath their words.

"Bath," one of them said — Lord Blackwell, I later learned — his voice rich as claret. "Though it tires me. The conversation, like the weather, wears thin."

I watched his eyes flick to me and linger — not rudely, but knowingly. A black cat contemplating whether to toy with a bird too tired to flee.

"It is necessary," said a shorter man beside him — Greene, with restless fingers and a silver watch chain that he touched compulsively. "Invitations, appearances. We can't all inherit our fortunes, can we? Some of us must negotiate."

"Negotiate," echoed another — Rathbone, I think — with a weary smile. His gloves were butter-soft and worn, the knuckles showing. "You make it sound like diplomacy."

"It often is," murmured Blackwell. "Wouldn't you agree, Miss—?"

Before I could answer, a voice coiled around me like silk.

"She agrees with whatever I do." I turned toward Edmund, bewildered.

"Gentlemen," he said, slipping an arm lightly around my waist, "Miss Alexandra Greystone. A lady of Penryn House. Remarkable. And *mine*."

The word struck like a chime. Mine.

I felt it in the roots of me — not possessive in jest, but possessive in claim.

"Ah she is yours, then?" Rathbone asked, with a flick of amusement. "I'm glad you made that very clear."

"Well, not yet," Edmund replied, raising his glass. "But I've every intention. I'd like to believe she looks the picture of a bride." I felt the blood rush to my face. Do they believe me to be deaf? Was I now invisible to them?

"Ah, wedding chimes on the horizon." Greene chuckled. "And here I thought you moved slowly in matters of the heart, Rothwell."

At that I took a sip — and nearly choked. The sweetness of my drink turned cloying, syrupy. Edmund only laughed and leaned close, almost nudging.

"She's reserved," he murmured, loud enough for them to hear. "But I'll have her say yes one day. Won't I, Alexandra?" His hand slipped to the small of my back once again. It felt not like affection, but orchestration—as though I were a marionette and he the one testing the string.

I swallowed, lowering my glass. Was this the man I had thought to know? The Edmund who had spun gold from charm and flattery? Was this manner he presented simply jest, or was it his true form—a man placing claims on women with the same ease of merely pouring a drink? Whatever the truth was, the taste of it now turned to ash in my mouth.

Blackwell's gaze caught mine — and held.

"A woman of spirit," he said. "Rare these days."

Blackwell shifted slightly, then offered a faint nod toward the empty armchair beside me—not with grandiosity, but with quiet assurance of a man who needn't lift a finger to be obeyed. I took a seat — carefully, as though the very act might bind me to some unseen bargain. A soul contract signed.

Edmund swallowed hard—still standing. "And rarer still to keep." Their laughter floated between them like perfume.

I could not breathe in the discomfort. And so instead, I smiled—thin, practiced, as mother had shown me—and steered the matter before the weight of it all crushed me.

"You reside in Bath?" I asked.

"Indeed," Blackwell said. "Business, mostly."

"Curious business," I said mildly, "for such varied company."

"Diversified interests," said Greene, too quickly, fiddling aimlessly at his watch.

"Tin," said Rathbone. "Trade. Men."

"Manpower," added Greene. "Cornwall has its uses."

"Such as?" I asked, meeting Blackwell's eyes.

He smiled, though nothing else shifted.

"—Forgive me," said Greene, clearing his throat. "It is merely commerce, Miss Greystone. Surely not a subject for—"

"Women?" I finished; my voice as sharp as a lace.

"Strange. We raise your future voters, soothe your wounded soldiers, survive your wars, and yet *commerce* is where you draw the line?"

A deafening silence fell. Greene's expression twitched.

"How about we discuss the commerce of women — how we're weighed, appraised, and promised like parcels at auction — all before we've said a word?"

I let the quiet stretch once more, sending not one glance in Edmund's direction.

"Or shall we speak of ribbons instead, if that's easier for you Mr Greene?"

The room stilled. A breath held, collectively — like the pause before glass cracks. Greene had gone slightly pale, his mouth parted as though searching for a reply he'd not rehearsed. He shifted in his seat, suddenly aware of his collar, his drink, the silence pressing in.

I had been in rooms like this before; not as a guest, not dressed in silk but in the corners, in the quiet, where words rang clearer than crystal.

My father thrived in this world. He would host small gatherings back home—nothing grand— a few men in tailored coats, voices low and serious. They would settle around the board with brandy and cards, not for the purpose of gambling, but for what came after.

Talk. Strategy. Names. Nations; the undercurrent of everything that moved the world forward or dragged it back. These evenings were not loud or raucous like the one before me—no, they were still, intense. The kind of stillness that lets a child hang onto every word.

And I had listened; from the stairwell, where the banister was warm from the day's sun. From the hallway, tucked behind a curtain or crouched at the hinge of a half-closed door. I had learned to breathe with quiet lungs and blink without sound. I could stay for hours—an invisible orb among living men.

That was how I came to understand the world— the world of cloak-and-dagger. Not taught through books or governesses, but through those evenings of brandy-laced truth and the iron weight of consequence. I learned how men discussed land, law, and the strategy of war. I learned what they feared, and how that fear shaped their votes, their marriages, their betrayals.

Lydia once caught me in the act; instead of scolding, she whispered, "Knowledge is armour, Tabby. If we are never given a sword, we must find another way to survive."

Her words have never left me, even into this lifetime.

Now, seated amongst these aristocrats, I recognised the cadence. The subtle barbs dressed in charm. The tug of power passed between glances. This was not new to me. I had lived my youth on the outskirts of such rooms, waiting to be let in. Now, I had arrived — not as the girl with her ear pressed to the wall, but as the woman with a voice, seated at their table.

Across from Greene, Lord Blackwell leaned back in his chair, watching me with something that might have been amusement — or calculation. The flick of his thumb against the rim of his glass was the only sound. He smiled, but not kindly.

"Fortunate," he said, "that you're more than merely lovely."

Edmund's arm stiffened. "She's clever," he said, but there was warning in his tone. "Too clever, perhaps."

"Do you have a wife joining you in Bath?" I asked suddenly. There it was — a flicker, the only break in Blackwell's resilient composure.

"Ah. Lady Blackwell would adore you. You two would get on famously. She has a mind for politics, too. And games."

My glass was near empty, my patience thinner still. But I smiled — not because I meant to, but because it was the only weapon I had left.

"I'm not very good at games," I said.

Blackwell inclined his head. "That's what makes you dangerous."

Beside me, Edmund's hand twitched.

"You'll forgive us," he said then, voice warm but brittle. "Alexandra prefers the quieter corners of society. The politics bore her."

"They don't," I said, without looking at him. Silence followed — then the soft clink of glass.

I sipped, I smiled and wondered if I had just met the men who would decide whether I survived the season.

The violins struck a livelier measure, and before I could rise on my own, Edmund was already at my side. His hand closed firmly around my waist.

"Excuse us gentlemen."

With practiced ease he steered us into the throng, his confidence cutting cleanly through the press of bodies, while I stumbled after — half led, half dragged — as though tripping over the wreckage left in our wake. We reached the floor at last — Edmund's left hand pressed firmly against my back, his right enclosing mine with practiced precision. Hesitantly, we found the rhythm, spinning into it until we blurred with the others — just another pair, indistinguishable, safely absorbed.

The tang of ash pierced my tongue once more.

❖

I had not danced so in years — if ever. The world whirled about us, candlelight and laughter dissolving into a blur, leaving only the surety of Edmunds steps, the strength of his hold. For the span of a song, it was almost easy to forget everything but the sweep of silk across the floor. The tension seemed to ease; the words once spoken by the hearth quietly consumed by flame. Forgotten, as all inconvenient things are in this society. But when the music lulled, when I caught my breath and looked across the glittering expanse of the room — that was when I saw *him*. *Stockholm.*

He stood apart, near the shadowed arch of a doorway. No glass in his hand, no card, no companion. His dark coat was severe against the brightness around him, his top hat now set aside. His face was half-lit by the chandelier's spill, and his gaze was fixed upon me.

As Edmund steadied me, I became aware of voices just behind us—young women, their tones quick with excitement, hushed with scandal, yet bright with laughter.

"Alaric Stockholm," one breathed, her giggle betraying nerves.

"A bachelor still. My father says he has the means to arrange a betrothal." Another girl sighed audibly.

"Imagine being Mrs. Stockholm."

Soft laughter followed; the kind sharpened by envy. The name clung to me; every syllable weighted.

Alaric.

A name of stone and steel, yet strangely elegant on the tongue. A hint of something hot and unfamiliar twisted in me as I listened to their chatter. Jealousy — sharp and unwelcome — at the thought of these girls daring to picture him beside them. Their foolish giggles brushed against my nerves, but he, he was not laughing. His eyes were still on me, unblinking, as though none of their talk had reached him, or perhaps because it had.

The line of his jaw was taut, his expression unreadable to those who did not know how to look — but I felt it, as though his stare pressed against my very skin. My breath caught, the music and laughter suddenly distant. Edmund's hand tightened gently at my waist, steadying me.

"You are pale — is it too warm?"

I forced a smile, but my eyes betrayed me, drawn back, again and again, to the figure in the shadows. Edmund led me from the floor, his hand still firm at my waist, and I let it linger there longer than propriety might approve. A smile — too sweet, too deliberate — curved my lips as I caught sight of Alaric's stare across the room. If he thought me blind, he was mistaken. I tilted my head toward Edmund, drawing close enough that a lock of hair brushed against his cheek as I whispered some pleasantry, laughing low as though he alone had earned my delight. Edmund's answering smile was wide, easy — but the tightening of Alaric's jaw across the room was what thrilled me most. I felt reckless. Dangerous. As though this was a game I had no right to play, and yet could not stop myself from indulging.

Each time I glanced across the hall, Alaric was there. His eyes followed, burning, unyielding. He stood with others now, a lady at his side speaking eagerly to him, yet his gaze never wavered. Edmund, oblivious to the undercurrent, grew only more attentive, more assured.

It was intoxicating, this dangerous push and pull. To see the cracks in his mask, to wield, if only for a moment, some power against the man who had haunted my nights for many moons. Yet even as I played the part, even as I leaned closer to Edmund and let the champagne sparkle upon my tongue, my pulse quickened for reasons I dared not name. For every look I cast toward Alaric, every flicker of his jealousy, was a reminder that he was not untouched. That he *felt* something, and I hated myself for wanting it.

The music amplified again, violins singing above the hum of conversation, but my smile faltered.

"Would you grant me the next, Alexandra?" Edmund tested. "It would be unpardonable to let the evening pass without one more dance."

I hesitated—but only for a breath. I could not afford to falter. I placed my gloved hand in his and the dance began, all soft turns and orchestrated elegance. His grip was practiced, his movements precise, yet I felt no steadiness in it now. I moved beside him, but my mind wandered— toward the colonnade, where I had seen his figure half-swallowed in shadow.

The music shifted—A partner change was required. I turned, and found myself facing—Lord Blackwell. His hand took mine with cool confidence, and as he stepped into place, a scent coiled around him. Bergamot, leather, iron. Not cologne, exactly—but a presence, sharp enough to engrave memory. He bowed slightly, the ghost of amusement playing at his mouth.

"You look as though you're dancing through a battlefield, Miss Greystone," he began, voice low, amused.

I met his gaze. "That depends. Which side am I on?"

He smiled, one brow arching. "Whichever makes the better game."

But before I could form a reply, my gaze drifted past his shoulder—and caught Edmund's. Though partnered with another, he was no longer attending to her. His gaze was fixed on me, burning with a heat he did not bother to conceal. There was no affection in it—only ownership. And the slow, barely perceptible tightening of his jaw. Blackwell spoke again, but his words blurred.

The steps shifted again.

Edmund was before me once more, his hand claiming mine with a touch that was no longer gentle. His fingers pressed firmly, a quiet reprimand in the form of a waltz — as though he meant to keep me turning in his grasp forever.

And then—Alaric was there.

He entered the floor as if summoned by my very heartbeat, moving with quiet precision into the next sequence. No announcement, no warning, but his presence was unmistakable. For a single moment, our eyes met.

Step.

Turn.

Their faces circled me—Blackwell, Edmund, Alaric—each a knight on some invisible board. And I—I stood at the centre. Not a queen. Not a player.

A piece.

The air thickened. The music thundered in my chest. My gloves felt too tight and the corset pressed too hard against my ribs. I could not breathe. I could not think. Edmund's hand held fast at my back, his lead unyielding. I moved because I had to — because the floor demanded it, because escape would cause a scene.

And then, from somewhere near the hearth, a voice rang out above the swell of violins — sharp, triumphant, final.

"Checkmate!"

The word struck through the room like a blade through silk. A few guests roared, the music carried on. To me, it felt as though the air itself had stopped — suspended between that one word and the hand that refused to let me go. I pulled back from Edmund, forcing a smile that trembled at its edges. My legs faltering.

"Forgive me, Edmund. The air—it overwhelms me. I must step aside, just for a moment."

His brow furrowed, his worry plain.

"Have I done something? You've grown pale—"

"No," I said quickly, placing my hand upon his arm with as much assurance as I could muster. "Never you. I only need a moment's rest. I shall return."

Reluctantly, he let me go, though his eyes followed with that quiet anxiety that had threaded all his letters. I turned, slipping into the corridor beyond the ballroom, where the air cooled and the noise dulled into a muffled hum.

❖

My skirts whispered against the marble floor as I searched for the powder room, eager to breathe, to banish the storm from my chest. For a moment, I simply stood there; one hand braced against the wall, the other taming my racing heart. The music behind me still played—muted now, like something heard underwater. My pulse overpowered it; echoing between my ears like footsteps in an empty hall. Shadows climbed the high walls, drawn long by candlelight. The stone beneath my hand was cool, solid, real. I let my head fall back against the wall and closed my eyes. But I was not alone.

A figure shifted from the shadowed recess between two velvet drapes. Tall, dark, his presence filled the narrow space with suffocating ease. Alaric's dark eyes met mine.

"Running from him already?" His voice was low, smooth, touched with mockery, yet threaded with something deeper. Desire, perhaps—or danger.

I froze. "You—"

He stepped forward, not abruptly, but with that slow inevitability I had come to dread. The curtain brushed against my shoulder as it fell back into place behind him, sealing us into a still and golden hush. His hand rose—not to touch, not quite—but near enough that I felt the heat of him, the hum beneath the air.

"Do you think I have not noticed?" His gaze burned into mine harder, unyielding. "The way you look at me. The way you turn away too late."

Anger flared in me, sharp and wild. "You flatter yourself. Whatever game you think you are playing, end it now. I want no part in it."

He didn't flinch. But the faintest shift in his gaze betrayed him—not wounded, but earnest.

"Then why do you run?" he asked, voice softer now. "If I truly meant nothing to you?". His head tilted, his eyes tracing the line of my cheek, the fall of my curls against my bare collarbone.

"You have not left my thoughts. I cannot sleep without seeing your face. You've taken root inside of me, Alexandra."

The sound of my name in his mouth sent a shiver racing through me. I pressed back against the wall, willing my body not to betray the tremor that passed through it.

"You are disgraceful," I whispered. "Stay away from me." He did not close the distance further, but the curtain narrowed the space between us. His presence—his scent, like spice and storm and something darker—coiled around me.

"Alexandra?" Edmund's voice rang down the corridor, taut with concern. The sound of my name unhinged me.

At once, Alaric reached for me—not forceful, but quick. I was pulled, sudden and silent, into the folds of velvet drapery. The fabric closed about us like a shroud, muffling the music and laughter into the beyond. My back pressed into the cold wall, and Alaric Stockholm stood so near I could feel the warmth of his breath against my cheek.

"Please—" he whispered, his bare hand covering my mouth. Not like the chill of a gloved palm; skin that was warm, unyielding and electric.

"Stay."

The curtain's heavy folds brushed against my bare shoulder, the faint musk of dust and candle wax filling my lungs. I tried to turn my face away, but he leaned closer, his forehead nearly grazing mine. His breath came rough, urgent, yet his voice was low, pleading. For a heartbeat, no more, the world outside ceased. His presence consumed the narrow space, the rise and fall of his chest so close it nearly matched my own. I felt his restraint, the tremor in his hand where it pressed against my lips, as though he were waging war against himself. Then, with agonising care, his hand slipped away. His fingers brushed the curve of my jaw, trailing down my neck, then to my arm. His touch was soft, and his skin was warm — too warm — against the sting of my torn flesh—

He stilled. His eyes instantly darkened.

"What is this?" he breathed. "Who did this to you?" His voice dropped lower still, laced with something near fury. "He is dangerous, Alexandra. Stay away from him."

I flinched, the heat of his words striking as hard as his nearness. My chest tightened; my breath unsteadied.

"You dare!" I pushed against him with both hands, though his body yielded with maddening slowness.

"You dare speak of danger? You did this. You. Stay away from me."

His eyes widened with genuine confusion flickering inside — even hurt. He looked as though I had struck him, and for a fleeting instant, he seemed less a predator and more a man undone.

"Alexandra!" Edmund's voice came again, nearer now. The spell broke. Alaric stepped back just as Edmund rounded the corner, his expression stricken. He rushed to me, seizing my hands as though to anchor me.

"My God," he murmured, his thumb brushing over my cheek. "You are shaking. What has happened?".

His gaze darted to the drapes, then to Alaric. Suspicion tightened his features, but he asked nothing more. Instead, he pressed a hand to my back, urging me forward.

"Come. You must wait in the carriage. I will not have you suffer in this hovel a moment longer." He flapped his other hand to shoo the world away. I let him guide me out, my limbs unsteady, my skin still burning where Alaric's fingers had grazed. The air of the ballroom struck me like heat after cold, suffocating in its brightness. Edmund shielded me from curious eyes, leading me swiftly through the doors and out into the night.

The carriage lanterns flared, throwing light upon his features as he lifted me inside. He kissed my knuckles with trembling urgency, his voice low but resolute.

"Stay here. I shall return shortly."

And then the door slammed shut, leaving me alone with my heaving breath and the ghost of Alaric's bare hand against my skin.

Chapter Fifteen

I do not know what passed in those shadowed halls once I had been shut away. The minutes dragged in silence, save for the restless snort of the horses and the faint creak of carriage wood. My hands would not still; they twisted the ribbon at my wrist until it nearly frayed, my mind circling back again and again to the heat of Alaric's touch, the words he had spoken — dangerous, Alexandra — as though they were meant to save me.

When at last the carriage door opened, Edmund stepped inside. Yet something in him had changed. The warmth that so often lit his features was absent. His mouth was drawn tight, his eyes dark with a hardness I had not seen before. Even the set of his shoulders seemed altered, rigid with some unseen weight.

"Are you well?" he asked — but his voice was clipped, too sharp to soothe.

"I... yes," I whispered, though my voice trembled. "I only felt faint. Forgive me."

His gaze lingered on me a moment too long, searching, probing, as though he doubted the truth of my words. Then, with a sound low in his throat, he sat back against the seat, his gloved hand rapping once against the carriage wall to signal the driver onward.

We lurched into motion. The air between us thickened. I felt his eyes upon me, not tender now but blackening, restless. His hand reached for mine; not with the gentleness of before, but firmly, almost possessively, his fingers tightening until the bones in my hand ached.

"You vanish from me in a crowd, pale and trembling, and yet you say nothing is amiss." His voice, though hushed, carried a rough edge that set my pulse racing. "Do you take me for a fool, Alexandra?"

I pulled slightly against his grip, but he did not release me. His gaze flickered to my face, softened for a heartbeat, then hardened once more, as though he fought some inner battle.

"I would protect you," he said at last, his tone low, fierce. "But you must not keep secrets from me. Promise me that you will not."

The night outside pressed black against the glass, the clip of hooves on cobblestone sharp in the silence that followed. My heart beat loud in my ears. I could not speak.

His grip did not loosen. Instead, he leaned nearer, the lantern light from the window catching in his eyes, making them gleam sharp as cut steel.

"You belong in no shadow," he said, each word measured, deliberate. "Yet you disappear into corners, allow yourself to be frightened like some trembling bird. I cannot—will not—stand by and watch it." His thumb pressed against the inside of my wrist, the pressure enough to send a tremor through me. I tried to draw breath, to steady myself.

"You hurt me," I whispered. The words slipped out before I could catch them. For a moment, his face changed — a flicker of remorse, almost boyish, passing over his features. He released my hand abruptly, as though scorched by my words, and turned his gaze to the dark glass of the window.

"You must understand," he said after a long silence, his voice rougher now, almost raw. "When I saw you falter — when I thought you might be lost to me — something in me— broke. I *cannot bear it*, Alexandra. The thought of you slipping away from me."

The horses' hooves rang steady against the road, the sound filling the carriage like a drumbeat. His shoulders rose and fell as though he wrestled with some storm inside himself. At last, he turned back to me, softer now, though the shadow of his earlier severity lingered. His gloved hand lifted, hovering near my cheek, but he stopped short of touching me.

"Forgive me," he murmured. "I am not myself tonight." The sincerity in his tone was real — yet the memory of his tight grip, the glint in his eyes, would not release me. I nodded, but my chest ached with unease. We rode the rest of the way in silence, the carriage swaying gently, the night pressing in like a shroud. Edmund's presence loomed beside me — steady, protective, and yet—unyielding. I then wondered, not for the first time, if even saints grow fangs beneath their prayers.

Chapter Sixteen

It had been nearly a month since the gathering at Hawkstone Manor, since the carriage ride, since I asked Edmund for space. I had spoken the words with shaking lips, and to my surprise, he had obliged. There were no visits, no letters, no soft knocks at the door. At first, I was grateful. Then uncertain. And now — now I could not tell if his silence was respect, or a punishment. Whatever it was, it left me restless.

That was why I found myself outside again at an hour when most of the house still slept. I liked the quiet, the stillness of the world before it dressed itself in noise. Today I went further than usual, through the fields and along the valley path, as if distance itself could put my thoughts in order. I laughed under my breath when I realised where my wandering had carried me. The faint outline of Marrowhall rose on the horizon. Even without intention, I had found myself drawn to it — as though the place pulled at me, the way a tide pulls at the shore. At the edge of the forest, movement caught my eye.

The stag.

The very same creature that had steered my path weeks ago; its coat shimmered bronze in the dappled light, each breath ghosting in the cool dawn air. I stepped forward, slow and unhurried, the earth soft beneath my boots—the scent of moss and wild thyme rising where I trod. A hush fell through the glade as though the forest itself had turned its gaze toward us.

The creature raised its head. Sunlight slipped across the curve of its neck, tracing gold over muscle and velvet fur. For a heartbeat it simply looked at me—not with malice, nor even with caution—only that deep, measured calm that belongs to things untouched by human cruelty. Then, with a grace that stilled the very air, it dipped its crown of antlers in a slow, deliberate bow.

I froze, breath catching. The first time we met, I had trembled in fear—but here, now, the gesture felt almost benevolent. The light deepened around us, pooling like liquid honey. A butterfly drifted behind, its wings glancing through the haze as though drinking in the sun itself. The air shimmered with salt — faint particles carried inland from the sea, catching the light and fracturing it into dusted gold, like breath made visible.

The moment taught me that perhaps not every threat was truly a threat—if one only slowed long enough to see it differently. And when I looked again, the stag's dark eyes held something achingly familiar. In them, *I saw him*—the same quiet strength, the same shadow restrained by grace.

It felt like an omen, a blessing perhaps, though of what, I could not tell. Around me, the forest stirred—as if Cornwall herself had drawn a long, knowing breath, and, in her ancient mercy, chose to let me belong. I wanted to remain there —to let the moment sink into me—but I knew that to respect beauty is to appreciate it from afar, to leave it untouched.

A soft wind rose from the valley, warm and coaxing, brushing my hair from my face as though to remind me where I was meant to go. It carried the scent of salt and sunlight, of something waiting—something calling me home. After a few strides, the valley opened before me; a cascade of green and golden, the river winding toward the sea. If I had never seen the ocean before, I would never have believed it carried waves — its surface lay smooth as glass that morning, like the world holding its breath.

I raised a hand to shield my eyes from the sun and paused—my gaze swept the breadth of the valley, until it found *him*.

He stood beneath the shade of a sycamore tree, coat tossed aside, an easel set before him. He bent over the canvas, paintbrush moving with quiet precision. Even from here, I recognised him. The cut of his shirt, open at the throat, the deliberate, easy posture — casual, yet undeniably refined.

Alaric.

I hadn't meant to approach, but the breeze carried me forward—gentle as a promise. One foot in front of the other. Then, too quickly, almost as if it broke me out of a spell, my boot caught in the long grass—I pitched forward with an undignified yelp, crashing onto my palms. Heat rushed to my cheeks. Please God, tell me he hadn't heard me.

When I scrambled upright, he was already standing before me, brush in one hand, the other set to his hip. His face was flushed with sun and the effort of his work, a sheen of sweat across his temple.

"Alexandra," he said. "What a pleasant surprise."

There was no mockery in his tone. If anything, he seemed almost—amused. I dusted at my skirts, flustered. "You paint? — out here?"

"Sometimes" he said, tilting his head slightly. "When the light behaves. Though I find it rarely does."

"You chase it anyway?" I asked, though I wasn't certain if I meant the light, or the thing that drove him to follow it.

He smiled faintly. "What else is worth chasing?"

His easel stood just behind him; the canvas turned away. I tilted my head, unable to resist.

"May I?"

He hesitated, brush tapping against his palm, then gave a small nod. As I approached the easel, I expected to see hills, trees, the river below. But it was not the valley at all.

It was hands. A series of studies — a child's soft palm reaching upward, a woman's fingers folded in prayer, a man's scarred knuckles. Each one rendered with startling tenderness, as though he had lived with those hands for a lifetime.

"You don't paint faces," I said softly.

"Faces lie," he replied. "They are practiced, trained, full of masks. Hands rarely bother to pretend."

"And what do mine say, then?" I tested, before I could stop myself. He looked down at them — folded before me, half-hidden in the fabric of my gown. His gaze lingered just long enough to make my breath catch.

"They say," he murmured, "that you carry more than you are willing to speak of."

I swallowed. "That sounds uncomfortably close to the truth."

His eyes softened. "Then forgive me. I did not mean to wound."

"You did not," I said quickly, almost too quickly.
A silence followed, the kind that seemed to stretch without breaking. Then, with sudden gravity, he set his brush aside.

"Alexandra," he said, "I owe you something. An apology —for what happened at Hawkstone — For the words I threw like stones. I have a talent for poor impressions."

I blinked at him, stunned.

"You admit as much?"

"Reluctantly" he said, the corner of his mouth lifting as he spoke. The tension in me eased.

"Well, perhaps not entirely poor."

His brows arched. "Not entirely?"

"You left me curious," I admitted. "That is a kind of success. And please—call me Alex."

He gave a low laugh — not mocking, but warm, almost boyish. "Then I will take it—*Alex*."

The way he said it — soft, certain — settled through me like warmth after a chill. It was only a name, my own, yet on his tongue it sounded altered somehow, gentler. For a heartbeat, I forgot the distance I had meant to keep.

He knelt to retrieve a rag from the grass, but looked up again as he did, eyes catching mine. "It is rare to find someone who refrains from scolding me."

"Perhaps you've been scolded often enough."

"Perhaps I deserved it."

A laugh escaped before I could stop it.

❖

We lingered there, speaking idly. Minutes, perhaps hours slipped by as though time itself had softened its grip. Eventually seated, cushioned by the soft grass beneath, the valley stretched quiet around us, the sycamore spreading its shade like a shelter. I surprised myself by laughing again — fuller this time, unguarded. Alaric tilted his head, eyes narrowing with a pleased sort of curiosity.

"You laugh easily, when you allow yourself to," he said.

"My father could make me laugh, only when he didn't try." I replied, already smiling at the thought. "Once, he decided to take the little boat out upon our pond — insisted he'd only meant to clear the lilies." My smile grew as I spoke, "Naturally, he leaned too far and went straight in—I can still see him floundering among the reeds, cigar clamped firmly between his teeth, as though keeping it alight might somehow preserve his dignity."

The image overtook me; I broke off, laughing outright. "Oh, the expression on his face — so utterly outraged, as though the water itself had plotted it. He insisted he'd meant to 'test the depth'." Oh, how I missed him.

Alaric chuckled low in his throat. "I cannot picture you laughing at such a scene."

"Then perhaps you do not know me at all," I said, though my smile faded quickly. I had nearly gone further

— nearly spoken of my sisters, of the way they shrieked and chuckled that morning, of how we had teased Father for weeks afterward. The words hovered, dangerous, and I swallowed them down. Tabitha was gone. Alex mustn't falter.

The wind now moved gently through the long grasses, carrying with it the scent of earth and distant salt. We had sat for some time without speaking, the hush between us not uncomfortable, but contemplative—like the pause before turning a page. Moments later, I stirred.

"I find I prefer it here," I whispered. "Removed from the town. There is a weight to its streets— a heaviness I cannot seem to shake."

Alaric did not look at me, but I felt the stillness in him shift—an attentiveness, silent and complete. I continued; my gaze fixed somewhere beyond the horizon.

"There is too much sorrow, too many eyes hollowed by hunger. I pass them by—those in rags, in threadbare boots, children with cheeks drawn pale from want—and I do nothing." My hands twisted lightly in my lap. "What can I do? I am neither wealthy nor titled. I possess no vote, no voice." My breath caught faintly. "I cannot help but feel the world is unspeakably cruel." I turned my head, almost in defiance. "Forgive me, I sound foolish." I brushed my skirts as if shame had left a stain.

Alaric didn't respond right away. He was watching me, the way someone watches a flame catch — not with pity, but admiration.

"You do not," he said softly. "You sound like someone who sees the world clearly— and still wants to make it a better place."

I looked away; my throat tight.

"My mother was much the same," he said, his eyes turned toward the valley. "She believed the world could be better — kinder. Not through grand speeches or force, but by lessening suffering wherever she found it, even in small corners. Even in silence—"

He flinched, as if it hit a nerve. "—she stood against cruelty. Her kindness was not loud, but it had direction —

a steady hand, a level mind, always turned toward what was just."

My breath stirred the loose curls near my cheek.

"She sounds lovely."

"She was." The words fell gently, but with a finality that held sorrow in its wake. His voice did not tremble, nor did he cloak the grief—it simply lived in him, steady as the wind.

"They died," he added after a pause. "Mother and Father. Drowned in a carriage accident."

Oh Alaric. I lowered my gaze. "I am sorry."

He plucked a stem of grass and turned it slowly between his fingers.

"She would have been very fond of you," he added. "She had little patience for vanity, but she admired courage. Especially the quiet kind."

A hush followed, deep and strangely warm. The sycamore murmured above us like some ancient witness, and the light shifted on the fields below—no longer harsh, but golden, tender. Though I told myself not to press him, the instinct to reach across the silence — to offer some small comfort — would not be stilled. I looked down at my hands, fingers curled faintly in my lap, as though they too carried the weight of remembrance— of grief.

"When I miss someone," I said softly, "I write to them. Letters, inked with the words I never had the chance to say—confessions I regret never whispering out loud, and the stories they were never granted the grace to write, to hear, or to live. I write them not for closure, but for offering — that they might, through something tangible, know the life I've lived in their absence. That they might find breath in ink, and footsteps in every phrase."

I raised my open palms to my chest, eyes closed now.

"I hold them close — As though the warmth might press meaning so deeply it slips between worlds, into the quiet where souls can listen — and then I burn them. The flames become prayer. The ashes— a messenger."

He turned, slowly, as if my words had drawn him from far away. "You burn them?"

I nodded. "So the wind might carry what my heart cannot. I do not believe the dead or lost are deaf, Alaric. Only that we must speak differently to be heard."

A pause. The hush between us thickened — not with sorrow, but with something solemn and tender.

"That is beautiful." His voice responded, scarcely above a breath. I looked up. His gaze held no pity, only wonder.

"Thank you," he breathed.

I could see it in his eyes; a recognition, perhaps, that pain, when shaped gently, could become a bridge between the living and the lost. He looked at me not as the world does, but as a man looking through a window into my soul.

The weight of it pressed into my chest.

I felt warmth rise — and then, just beneath it, fear. Not of him. Of what he might come to mean.

Of what I can't bear to lose.

"Lady Hawthorne will be worried," I said, preparing myself to stand.

Alaric rose. "I shall take you."

He gave me no chance to protest, and moved with quiet efficiency; gathering his belongings with the care of a man who had long learned the worth of preparedness. A coil of rope, a worn leather satchel, a folded cloak — all placed with purpose into the saddle. His hands were sure but never rushed, every gesture deliberate, as though the horse were part of the ritual rather than merely the bearer of it.

When at last he turned to the mare, the sharpness that so often clung to him seemed to soften, dissolving like mist in morning light. He pressed his forehead to the hollow between her eyes, his arms circling her head as though she were not a beast but an old friend, a confidante. The horse stilled under his touch, her lashes fluttering once before settling, her breath easing into a steady rhythm. A quietness seemed to move through her, spreading from the crown of her head to the heaviness of her shoulders.

His hand drifted down the length of her neck, fingers tracing the sleek muscle beneath the glossy coat, before patting her shoulder with an affection that was certainly devotion. It startled me—this tenderness. Men I had known wielded strength as a weapon but here, Alaric was offering something wordless and unwavering, something I had not believed could exist: kindness without demand — loyalty without cost. My throat tightened. The world shifted in that moment, as if I were glimpsing him anew.

Before I knew it, he was next to me. With a considerate gesture, he helped me onto his horse— steadying me with one hand at my waist, careful but firm. When he swung up behind me, I felt the warmth of him, the safety of his presence.

"Take the reins," he uttered, his voice low near my ear. "She'll trust you, if you trust her. Horses understand us better than we understand ourselves."

❖

The ride back was quiet, but not strained. At one point I looked over my shoulder — just briefly — and found him watching me. My stomach turned over, though I quickly faced ahead. A smile cradled the side of my cheek.

Before I knew it, the familiar silhouette of Penryn House crested into view. Its quiet presence a balm against the horizon. Yet as it drew nearer, a sadness stirred in my chest — soft, but certain — for the day was ending, and with it, the strange, aching nearness of Alaric. The gravel crunched beneath the hooves as we reached the front steps. He brought the horse to a halt, dismounted swiftly, then turned to extend a hand.

"Careful," he murmured.

I placed my hand in his, meaning only to steady myself, but as I slipped down he caught me at the hips — firm, certain, unhurried. For a breath, the world felt suspended: his warmth through the thin fabric of my gown, the scent of leather and earth, the soft exhale between us that was neither mine nor his alone.

Then he released me, and the absence felt louder than the contact alone. The air rushed back; the moment folded in on itself, neat as a secret returned to its hiding place. I then noticed a pale curtain stirred in one of the upper windows, as if my boots touching the earth created a breeze.

I turned back to him then, uncertain whether to speak. He had already lifted back into the saddle, one hand resting on the reins, the other on his thigh, gaze unreadable beneath the brim of his hat. For a moment, we simply looked at one another — not quite farewell, not quite anything at all. Then he gave me the faintest nod. Not cold, but final. Without a word, he beckoned his horse and rode back along our trail. His silhouette was soon swallowed by the dip of the valley, until only wind and gravel remained in his wake — and that quiet, unnameable fear that comes when presence turns to memory.

Chapter Seventeen

It became, before we knew it, a ritual. Each morning, while the rest of Penryn House stirred itself awake, I slipped away into the quiet. By the time Lady Hawthorne rose and asked for me, Una would set the tea and mutter some gentle excuse on my behalf.

The valley awaited me, wide and hushed, the sycamore standing sentinel where the meadow curved. And, as though by fate's mischievous hand, he was always there. Sometimes he was already seated at his easel, brush poised with impossible precision. Other mornings he lounged against the tree itself, sketchbook balanced lazily upon his knee. On rarer days, he would arrive after me, his mare's hooves muted by the long grass; his greeting no little more than a tilt of his head, as though to acknowledge that we had met once again at the same hour, in the same place.

We never spoke of arranging it. We never confessed to waiting. And yet, the meeting became inevitable, as much a part of the day as the rising of the sun. The days began to collect like beads upon a string.

One morning, I carried a small basket with bread and fruit, and we shared it beneath the tree. Alaric peeled an apple with careful precision, passing me slices as though it were the most natural thing in the world. He teased me gently for eating so daintily, and I teased him back for eating like a soldier, and before long the air was light with laughter.

Another day, he turned his canvas toward me and asked, with disarming frankness, if I would sit. Flustered, I obeyed, folding my hands in my lap as he observed me in silence. When he revealed the work at last, I found not my face, but my hands rendered in startling tenderness. I had to look away, for fear of what he had seen in them that I had not.

It was on the next day, he allowed me his brush.

"Your turn," he said, extending it toward me with a wry, almost careful smile. I made an appalling attempt at painting his likeness, and he endured it with mock seriousness until I ruined the image entirely by sketching the most ridiculous moustache across his face. He laughed then, too, though quieter, watching me as though the act itself pleased him more than the result.

Once, rain surprised us. We huddled beneath the tree as the drops fell heavy, and Alaric shrugged out of his coat to cast it about my shoulders. By the time the clouds passed, both of us were damp, laughing at the absurdity of it, skin frozen and garments clinging.

That was the moment I'd realised that in the scramble, my hair, traitorous in the damp, escaped its pin and had clung in dark clumps of ringlets across my cheek and brow. With impatient hands I tried brushing it back, but the more I fought, the worse the tangle became, until one stubborn curl fell directly over my nose. It was the first time I saw him laugh — not a sardonic smile, not a restrained smirk, but a true, full-bodied laugh that shook through him like music. I must've looked a spectacle. My own cheeks warmed despite the cold.

"It is not amusing Alaric!" I shouted, trying once more to wrestle the rebellious shrouds of hair behind my ear, only for it to spring forward again like a thing possessed.

He laughed harder, nearly breathless with his head tipping back, until at last he steadied himself against the tree.

"Forgive me — You are hopelessly besieged".

My cheeks flamed. Surrendering to the embarrassment of it, I collapsed my hands into my face and turned my head to hide— but he stepped closer. His hand lifted, hesitant at first, and he brushed the damp strands gently from my face. His fingers lingered only long enough to tuck the strand behind my ear. His touch paralysed me. I caught my breath, the world tightening around the moment. Something opened in me then, some chamber I had longed to be kept closed, and it frightened me how easily he'd found the key.

I did not look at him again that day. If I had, I feared that he would have seen more than he ever painted, more strokes on my palm to etch on his canvas. My hands now told a different story.

❖

The corridors of Penryn were hushed when I returned that day; the hush of a house that disapproved of noise. My boots left a trail of water across the marble — dark prints blooming and fading beneath each step. The air clung to me, thick with rain and adrenaline.

I could still feel it — the downpour on my skin, the sound of his laughter caught between thunderclaps. My hair had now come completely loose in wild strands; my gown clung close, heavy and cold, yet I had not the heart to care. For the first time in what felt an age, I was beaming. As I reached the base of the staircase, a sound drifted through the air — music, low and deliberate. Lady Hawthorne was at the piano.

From where I stood, I could see her through the open archway: upright, poised, her back a perfect line of discipline against the gleam of the instrument. Candlelight trembled along the polished keys. The melody — a sonata, perhaps — filled the hall with the kind of serenity that felt almost rehearsed. I climbed the first few steps quietly, not wanting to disturb her. But water slipped from my hem and struck the wood with faint, treacherous notes of its own.

She paused. The music faltered — not fully stopped, but suspended. Her head turned slightly, just enough for me to glimpse her profile in the dim. One glance — that was all.

A silent acknowledgment. And beneath it, the smallest quiver of disapproval.

Then, without a word, she returned to the keys. The melody resumed, colder now — precise, unyielding. I climbed on. Each step seemed to draw her playing sharper, as though the sound itself sought to scold me. By the landing, I could see my reflection in the stairwell mirror — hair darkened to near-black by the rain, cheeks flushed with life. I looked alive, not proper. Not the kind of woman she had been shaping.

She will never understand it, I thought. That something wild could be beautiful. That I could be both claimed by thunder and free.

The piano swelled again, a bright, brittle sequence chasing me up the final flight. I smiled faintly to myself, though my heart was still thudding from the storm — not the one outside, but the one I had walked straight into, and found I did not wish to escape.

Chapter Eighteen

And so the days passed, one folding gently into another— one bead after another, until time itself seemed held beneath that tree, caught between the valley and the river.

It was on such a day — when the weather was kinder, perhaps even warmer than most, the sky dappled with soft, cotton white clouds — I found myself stretched upon the grass, my head pillowed against his chest. He lay reclined, his arm loose at his side, fingers idly turning the stalk of a grass seed, twirling and twirling as though thought itself had taken form.

Above us, the sycamore bent its branches like a canopy, and beyond, the heavens stretched wide. His breathing was slow, steady, and without thought I matched my own to its rhythm. There was no strain between us. No caution. I felt utterly myself, as though my skin were no longer armour but simple flesh. He glanced down at me once, a half-smile tugging faintly at his mouth. No words passed between us, yet something softer, truer than words seemed to linger in the air — a mutual acknowledgment, a sweetness neither of us dared disturb. And yet, for fear of drowning wholly in the silence, I spoke.

"What did you mean," I asked carefully, "when you said Edmund was dangerous?"

The shift in him was immediate. His body stiffened, his chest tightening beneath my cheek. He sat up abruptly, brushing the grass from his sleeve as though to busy his hands. His expression, when I searched for it, was completely unreadable; as if staring at an iron wall.

"He has a temper," Alaric said at last. "And a way of bending others to it. He gets what he wants."

Nothing more. His voice was calm, but beneath it I felt the warning — sharp, unspoken.

I thought back, unbidden, to the carriage. To the moment when Edmund's eyes had glinted with something cruel, when I had felt my pulse caught beneath his command. I said nothing, only nodded, though the weight of it pressed cold against my chest. I decided to not press further on the matter.

For a moment neither of us spoke. The breeze shifted, stirring the grass. Then, as though the heaviness had troubled him too, Alaric reached for a small buttercup near his knee. He brushed the petals with his thumb, as though testing their softness, then leaned closer, the faintest smile at one corner of his mouth.

"Hold still," he murmured.

I obeyed without thinking. He lifted the flower to my chin, tilting my face toward the sun.

"What are you doing?" I asked, smiling despite myself.

"An experiment," he said. "If your skin glows yellow, it means you're fond of butter."

I laughed — a small, startled sound that felt like coming up for air.

"And if it doesn't?"

"Then I'll try again," he said, eyes bright with mischief.

I gave him a light nudge with my shoulder, half laughing, half warning. "You're insufferable."

"Undoubtedly," he said, grinning.

The tension between us finally eased, the heaviness scattered like pollen on the breeze.

With it, the day began to wane, and as the shadows lengthened, Alaric led me back. His horse carried us with the same steady rhythm as before, perhaps even slower this time; his presence at my back both protective and perilously close.

At first I sat upright, hands firm on the reins. But the motion of the horse, the warmth of the setting sun, and the steadiness of him behind me drew me gently backward. My shoulder brushed his chest, then my head, as though of its own accord, found its place just beneath his jaw. It fitted there as though it had always belonged. His breath stirred lightly against my hair.

Stillness fell — not awkward, but a heavy, exquisite kind. Then, as though compelled, his arm tightened gently about me, drawing me closer. The movement was not demanding, but steady, resolute — a sheltering hold that seemed to claim nothing yet gave everything. I turned my head fractionally, daring at last to meet him halfway. My temple brushed the line of his throat; my cheek lay against him, and in that nearness, I could almost believe the world beyond us had ceased to exist. His breath caught — almost unnoticeably — and his chin lowered the slightest degree, grazing the crown of my hair.

The air was thick with all that was unspoken, all that hovered just beyond reach. In that moment, I felt not fear, nor danger, but the unravelling of something far deeper, a feeling that promised to undo me completely.

I might have stayed in this embrace forever, had the roofline of Penryn House not broken in the twilight sky. When we reached the steps, he dismounted first, as he always did, turning to help me down. The gesture had become almost habitual — his hand extended, mine placed in his — a brief, wordless courtesy we both understood. I descended, expecting him to release me the moment my boots touched the stone. But he did not. His fingers lingered, steady, deliberate, and before I could question it, he bent — not deeply, not ceremoniously, but with a quiet grace that caught the breath from my chest. His lips brushed my hand — a touch so light it scarcely seemed real, yet it set every nerve alight.

The world contracted to that single point of contact: the rasp of his breath, the faint scent of rain and leather, the steady thrum beneath my skin that was not quite fear and not yet understanding. I stared at him, dumbfounded, my heart thudding in disbelief at the sudden betrayal of our ritual. It was only a kiss, no more than a breath — yet something in its simplicity undid me entirely.

He clasped my hand and held his gaze on mine,

"Some things can't be painted," he murmured. "Only felt."

❖

Closing the great oak door behind me, I leaned against it, breath caught, my pulse wild. The weight of it shuddered through the frame, the iron bolts groaning in their sockets as though they shared in my unrest. The wood was cool at my back, smelling faintly of wax and age, and I pressed myself into it as if its ancient strength might steady me.

My hand still pulsed where his lips had touched. I closed my eyes, surrendering for one dangerous instant to the memory — the warmth, the stillness, the perilous sweetness of it. But the silence fractured.

A blow struck the door just above my shoulder, violent enough to jar the hinges. My eyes flew open, heart leaping like a startled pheasant. Edmund.

His face was thunder, shadowed by a wrath that seemed to smoulder in his very bones. His eyes gleamed obsidian, riddled with rage, and his voice, when it came, was low and dangerous, frayed at the edges with fury.

"Where have you been? With *him*?"

The word *him* left his mouth like pure venom, spitting through the air between us. I drew in a breath, forcing my spine to straighten though my pulse rattled like a snare.

"He was painting. We spoke. He offered to see me home."

"You think I do not hear?" His hand pressed harder to the wood beside me, the veins taut, his knuckles white. "Do you know what people say? Do you know what they whisper?"

I lifted my chin, though fear prickled sharp along my skin. "I know what I have seen. I sense what you are capable of, Edmund. Others have called it temper." My voice caught, but I steadied it. "I call it something else."

His jaw clenched, the muscle ticking with barely bridled rage. For a dreadful moment I thought he might strike not the door this time — but me. His eyes scoured my face with such intensity, it was as though he sought to leave a bruise without even touching me. The silence between us thickened, oppressive as a storm waiting to break.

And then, with sudden violence, he wrenched the door wide. I pulled myself aside just in time, the air rushing cold past me as he stormed into the night. The door slammed behind him with a force that shook the hall to its core, leaving me alone in the quivering dark. The echo lingered, trembling through the floorboards, through my bones, until I could no longer tell where the sound ended and the silence began.

For a moment I stood paralysed — trembling, breath caught, my hands aching from how tightly I had held them at my sides in defiance. I wanted to vanish. I wanted to scream. It's nothing, compose yourself, I thought. There is no danger here. Only silence, only a door, only air. Yet my pulse would not heed me; it throbbed wildly, betraying every effort toward calm. I took one large breath, then slowly turned toward the staircase.

I knew that to stand still was to break.

Each step forward sent a hollow sound into the vastness, swallowed almost instantly by shadow. The portraits lining the walls seemed to watch as I passed — their painted eyes gleaming faintly in the candlelight, their mouths composed, indifferent. Not one seemed willing to intervene. Not one blinked. By the time I reached the first stair, I realised I was holding my breath. Then, came the sound.

The piano. Lady Hawthorne was playing. I could see her from this position, just as I did before. Her posture was immaculate, back straight, hair pinned to perfection — but her fingers moved differently now. The music was soft, hesitant. A simple, circular melody, the kind one plays to fill silence rather than to make it.

It was the sound of choosing not to hear. My steps on the stairs were unsteady. I caught the railing but my hand slipped; it was shaking too violently.

She did not turn this time. Not even to acknowledge me.

Just that same melody — placid, practiced, deliberately blind. Each note felt like a door softly closing —

a breath smothered,

a cry swallowed.

a bird's wing pressed still beneath an unforgiving palm. In that moment, it all came to me; this was the art of survival in such a house — to feign calm while the soul thrashed beneath. To keep the melody gentle, lest the truth disturb the air. I climbed the stairs slowly, every step heavier than the last. The walls seemed narrower than before, the air colder. Even the chandelier light felt dimmer, as though the house itself had drawn in to hide.

Once, I had climbed these same stairs drenched in rain, smiling. Now I climbed them drenched in dread, quivering.

When I reached the landing, I paused — waiting, hoping she might call after me. She did not. I turned away, tears stinging my eyes, and hurried down the corridor.

By the time I reached my chamber, I could no longer hear the piano. Only the echo of it remained — a polite, graceful kind of cruelty. I slammed the door behind me and pressed my back to it. My reflection met me in the mirror — pale, hollow-eyed, a creature half-consumed by the very house that had promised her safety; trapped in a bird cage of silk and silence.

I sank before the vanity, my knees folding as though my bones had turned to dust. The same single, lonely candle trembled before me. I reached for the brush — more out of pattern than purpose — and dragged it through my hair with trembling hands. Strand by strand, I tried to smooth the ruin. As if order could be found again in that mirror. As if dignity might be coaxed back with bristles and breath.

Then— a knock. Soft, cautious. I froze at the sound of it, still shaken, then wiped at my cheeks with the back of my hand.

She didn't push open the door, not fully. Only hovered — as if she sensed that tonight, more than most, space was something I clung to. The voice, when it came, was gentle, unstartling, "Shall I run you a bath, miss?"

I sighed—it was Una.

I couldn't speak at first. My throat ached from holding in the sobs, my pride more wounded than anything else. I swallowed, nodded — then found the strength for words.

"Please." The word scraped out of me.

The silence held. Not hollow, but full. And as her footsteps drifted away, I sat quietly before the mirror — tear-streaked, half-undone, a woman nearly broken by the hour. Then came the faint rush of water from the adjoining room — Una's quiet care, steady as faith itself. The sound was a balm, a promise of rescue amidst ruin. I exhaled, slow and trembling.

Thank the Heavens for her — my light in this house of shadows.

Chapter Nineteen

The night before lingered on me like a bruise. Edmund's anger had not left with his footsteps. It clung like smoke in drapery. I knew better today than to stir it further. And so, when the morning came and Una suggested attending a village for errands, I agreed — not for need, but to still my thoughts — and to escape. What I could not allow myself was to seek Alaric again. That would be folly. That would stoke a fire already too near the oil.

The morning was dull with a chalky sky, the air heavy with the tang of mist, like water stolen from a mountain spring. The road turned gently toward the neighbouring village; it was a simpler place than the markets we'd usually attend in Truro. The houses sat lower, their chimneys leaning slightly with age, their stone walls weathered by salt and sun.

Una walked beside me, her step light over the uneven cobbles, skirts brushing just above the dust. Her gown was of a plain dove-grey muslin, serviceable but neat, her apron fastened tightly as though the string were armour. There was no extravagance in her manner — she wore no ornament beyond the pin that held her cloak — yet she turned heads without ever seeming to ask for attention. A natural, effortless beauty.

The sunlight caught in her chestnut curls, which she had coiled neatly into a bun at her nape, soft tendrils escaping at her temples as though no pins could fully tame them. Her eyes — hazel, flecked with gold — moved constantly, taking in the world with quiet alertness, and yet rarely giving herself away. She was not much older than I was, not in years — but the weight she carried made her seem older all the same. There was something in her posture, in the calm restraint of her silence, that spoke of things endured. Hard things. Private things. And though she never spoke of them, they shaped her like weather shapes stone.

In another life, she might have been a lady. In yet another, something fiercer — a woman forged of both elegance and iron. She was not merely a maid. Not merely a companion. She had become, without ever asking for the title, something closer to a pillar — a quiet constant. Someone to steady me when I lost my footing. Someone I had come, quite without realising, to anchor my sanity to.

I wrapped myself in a slate-grey cloak, the hood drawn low, though Una fussed beside me in her dark-blue bonnet, her cheeks turning pale with some inner disturbance. The errand was simple enough—ribbons, bread, and a letter to be entrusted to the post—but her unease pressed upon me as we strolled deeper into the village, as though she feared the very air might betray us.

"I never remembered this place to be so — derelict." She whispered under her breath, as if the ghosts lost to this village — to its cliffs, its caves, its cursed waters — would claw their way out of the fog and drag her down with them.

It bore the marks of prosperity completely undone.

"In so little time" Una remarked, as if she could read my mind; her eyes scanning her surroundings. Not only fear embodied her complexion, but sorrow too. Stalls were laid out with limp fish and bruised apples. Here, the roofs had slumped, their slates patched with driftwood. Whole terraces leaned as though one sharp wind might topple them into rubble. Each cobbled street had an erratic bustle of need: men idling at corners, their boots worn through at the sole; children in tatters; women standing with baskets, their eyes hard as iron. It was not a place where one might walk untroubled, least of all two women alone.

Una clung to my arm with a nervous haste, though she tried to mask it with clipped remarks about the price of butter and the crooked scales of the fishmonger. My hood still shaded my face; yet still I felt the stare of too many eyes upon us, the hush that fell as we passed groups of men who had no business there but idleness.

It was one such group that rose from the alehouse door — four of them, broad in the shoulder, the smell of spirits clinging even in the morning air. Another two, rose from leaning against the opposite wall, sodden with soot. Their laughter was low, coarse, and meant for our ears alone.

"Pretty birds," one man slurred.

"Two fine ladies come to grace our poor street," another drawled, stepping into our path.

Una's grip on me tightened. I willed my step not to falter, though my pulse beat hard in my ears. We might have turned aside, had not another man moved to block the way, his grin splitting beneath unshaven cheeks.

Before I could speak, Una stepped forward — placing herself between me and them.

"Do not touch her."

She did not raise her voice, nor shrink from their gaze. There was something almost holy in her composure — the kind of stillness that makes even cruelty hesitate. Her chin lifted slightly, her shoulders squared, as though the daylight itself had drawn close around her, a quiet sentinel in her defence. For one suspended moment, she looked like the very embodiment of what these men could never touch — dignity, resolve, grace held in human form. Yet in the blink of an eye, the man seized her and flung her to the ground.

Then—steel rang through the air.

The men turned, and so did we.

A man stood before us, interposed in one fluid motion. He came through the mist as though it parted for him. A tall, broad-shouldered figure, his stride long and unhurried, yet there was an unmistakable weight to him— the kind of weight born from battle. He wore a coat of dark bottle-green wool, cut with the precision of a soldier's tailor, and beneath it a waistcoat of black-and-gold brocade that caught the pale light. His cravat was tied in a careless knot, as though he had no patience for the frippery, and at his hip gleamed the hilt of a blade.

"Gentlemen," he said lightly, though the smile that played on his mouth never reached his eyes.

"I'd suggest you step aside. Unless you'd care to discover how quick I am."

A moment's silence, then the men scattered like rats, scurrying back into shadow. The stranger proceeded to approach.

"Are you hurt?" he asked Una, whilst assisting her to her feet. She shook her head, though tears pooled at the corners of her eyes.

"Come," he gave the order easily, the word falling from his mouth like something long familiar — a habit rather than a demand. "This street is not fit for either of you."

His hair — sun-burnished chestnut, curling and falling just enough to soften the stern set of his shoulders. It was thick and slightly dishevelled — not by carelessness, but by a nature that refused to be tidied. His eyes, green flecked with ocean blue, seemed to hold both laughter and warning at once. Boots of polished black reached nearly to his knee, and the cut of his trousers betrayed a figure accustomed to the saddle, every inch the cavalryman even without the uniform.

Una began to weep, quietly but with enough energy that left her muddy skirt trembling in her hands. She had landed hard in the dirt, palms grazed, her apron streaked and the heel of her boot snapped clean. The villagers had watched in silence.

"She'll have me turned out, I know it —" Una sniffled, head down, brushing her skirts.

"Who? Lady Hawthorne?" I replied. The statement taking me back a step. I knew she was cold, fastidious perhaps, but I never thought her capable of wielding any true malice. Before the thought pressed further, I bent beside her, arms bracing her shoulder—I could feel her trembling beneath them.

"We can't go back yet, not with you like this Una". I pulled a handkerchief out of my skirts, and wiped her tears.

"Thank you, miss," her relief softened her features.

That is when the stranger leaned in, "I have a place—not far from here. You may take refuge. It belongs to Alaric Stockholm. I am in his service and believe he would wish it". His voice remained low, careful not to press. "No harm will come to you—you have my word."

Silence hung like a thread, stretched tight.

Another bead added to our string.

I looked at Una for approval, then nodded. His demeanour softened once more,

"James Rowe," he said simply, offering no bow, no flourish. Only a name that carried weight like a struck bell. Even in my sheltered circles, I heard the whispers of a soldier named James, famed for both charm and brutality in combat. I believe it was Alaric himself who first spoke of him beneath the sycamore; he had mentioned their years in the Crimea, half in recollection, half in regret.

Yet beside Una now, he possessed an energy as gentle as a golden retriever. It was strange, after hearing of those frozen battlefields, to see him now — all light and tenderness as though war had never known his name.

Chapter Twenty

Una sat beside me in silence, her face turned toward the window, though her reflection revealed more than she wished to show. Her lashes were still wet; a single tear clung stubbornly at her chin before she brushed it away.

Across from us sat James; he had the look of someone accustomed to command — shoulders broad beneath his coat, posture relaxed yet deliberate, as though every inch of stillness had been earned. An honest hand rested on his knee, fingers lightly interlaced; there was no arrogance in the pose, only a kind of quiet authority, the sort born of discipline rather than vanity.

I caught myself studying him — the cut of his jaw, the faint scar that ran from temple to cheek, the steadiness and warmth in his eyes. I imagined him beside Alaric in the war — the same composure under fire, the same unspoken trust that men build in the dark.

He must have felt my gaze, because his mouth curved into a faint, reassuring smile.

"Don't worry," he said lightly. "I don't bite."

Una's eyes flicked toward him, wary, though something softened in her expression at his tone.

"You've already done enough," she said quietly.

He tilted his head. "Only what anyone should." Then, after a pause, added, "Though not everyone would, I suppose."

There was a kind warmth in the words — a disarming one. The kind of man who could steady a frightened horse or a frightened heart, I thought, without changing his voice.

For a moment, silence settled — gentle, almost companionable. Then in the same breath, the carriage wheel struck a stone, jolting us sharply.

Una caught her breath. In the same instant, James's hand moved to the hilt at his side — not in aggression, but reflex, pure instinct. His body stilled, eyes scanning the hedgerows beyond the glass. It lasted only a heartbeat before he eased back again, the soldier gone as swiftly as he'd surfaced.

Una glanced at him — not fearfully, but with something close to understanding.

He offered a small, apologetic smile.

"Old habits," he reassured.

The corner of Una's mouth lifted, just barely.

"Then let's hope they're good ones."

Her tone carried the faintest spark — dry, composed, unexpected. I looked at her beside me, surprised, though I tried not to show it. Composure and wit rarely shared a face, yet there it was — the ghost of a smile cutting through the quiet like a blade through mist.

James's answering grin was boyish, golden, and for a moment the weight in the carriage eased.

The road narrowed as it bent uphill, curving through a long avenue of beech trees that arched above like the vaults of a cathedral. Pale morning light spilled through the leaves, dappled across the carriage as it rolled slowly forward. Mist clung to the ground in thin ribbons, wreathed around the wheels and licking at the horses' legs like fingers reluctant to let go.

Then, the trees broke — and the house revealed itself.

It stood in quiet majesty beyond a semicircle of hedged lawn and crushed stone paths, its façade pale gold, softened by age and the embrace of ivy that curled across its eaves. Long balconies ran the length of the upper floor, pillars framed the double doors, and above them, the tall windows shimmered with the last of the mist.

In the centre of the drive, a wide stone fountain gurgled steadily. A sculpted stag stood at its heart, antlers raised, water spilling from its hooves. The sound was tranquil — an invitation, a promise.

I leaned forward slightly, hand at the windowpane. I hadn't known what to expect — certainly not this. Not something so private and beautiful, tucked in a fold of the land like a secret.

"Trewyllow House," James said, his voice softer now, touched with something like pride. "He keeps this residence quiet," James continued. "Marrowhall belongs to the Stockholm legacy. This—this is where he breathes. Built long before Marrowhall—He prefers it here."

The carriage came to a halt. Two stable hands appeared without summons, taking the horses and pulling open the doors with brisk efficiency. James dismounted and offered his hand to Una. She took it reluctantly, though I saw the faintest colour return to her cheeks.

"Come Una," James beckoned. "You'll find peace here."

He then cast a look over his shoulder, directing his gaze towards me — mischief curling through his voice.

"He's with the horses." James' glance gestured to the far end of the manor, beyond the yew hedges and toward the stables nestled beneath the hill's crown.

❖

I walked alone.

The gravel faded into moss, where mist clung to the earth like breath upon glass, it curled and retreated as the morning warmed its edges. A row of black poplars lined the

130

path that led away from the House, their trunks silvery in the hush, their leaves whispering like the wind's quiet counsel. Somewhere behind me, the laughter of Una and James was swallowed by the garden's hush.

I followed the path where James had pointed, boots hushed by wet grass, my skirts damp at the hem. The stables to my right stood solemn and still, each stall empty, save for the sweet breath of hay.

No Alaric — Not even a groom. Only the silence of a place left willingly.

A beam of sunlight must've broken through the clouds in that moment, and pooled through the beams; casting long, golden rectangles upon the hay-strewn floor. The dust caught in them like ghosts, rising and falling in the hush. My eyes scanned the shadows; a bridle hung on a rusted nail, the leather darkened by use, the reins twisted neatly around themselves as if just removed. A saddle rested on the low rail, the same one — I was certain — that had sat upon Alaric's horse the day before.

There was still a smear of dried mud on the stirrup. An apple — bitten, its pale flesh browning — lay atop the feed barrel. The skin was still damp where teeth had broken it. I pressed a palm to the saddle — still warm.

A breath caught in my throat.

Then — a sound. The earth itself shuddered. I turned sharply, heart vaulting, and stepped past the wall, looking into the field afar.

Thunder rolled — not from the sky, but the ground. I stepped out into the opening fields, beyond the line of trees. The morning mist curled thicker there, rising in soft, ghostly plumes over the heathered ground. And from it emerged the herd.

Friesians.

Pitch black silhouettes surged through the misted valley, like smoke made flesh. Their manes flew wild, hooves tearing divots through the dew-wet grass. The air trembled with their power, with their rhythm, parting the mist around them as if the earth itself bowed to their beauty.

Towering and graceful, each horse moved with a fury and grace that stole the breath from my lungs.

A low cry slipped from my lips, unbidden.

They galloped like black fire over the moor, manes lashing, hooves striking like drums.

And among them — Alaric.

He ran with them. Not behind, not before — completely intertwined among them.

He darted with them, weaving between flanks and tails, laughing — freely, loudly — the sound ringing out like a bell in a monastery. One of the horses reared, and he ducked, his hand grazing its flank in a touch so natural it might have been breath itself. Another nipped playfully at his shoulder and he swayed away, only to pivot and run beside it, matching its gait with effortless rhythm.

His coat was discarded, flung somewhere unseen—His white shirt clung to him, soaked with mist and sweat, chest heaving. His dark hair streamed behind him, boots churned the sodden earth. He was not commanding them, nor fleeing them. He was part of them. The herd's breath was his breath; their wildness, his.

It was a vision.

It was not riding— not control— a dance. Man and beast, wild and willing, storm and stillness. No reins, no commands. Only instinct, only trust. The kind of trust born from long silences and open hands. I watched as he stretched his arms wide, unafraid, and the herd parted for him like a tide split by the moon.

My heart thudded. I could not name the emotion, only feel it swell — enormous and dizzying — until my eyes stung. This was Alaric as I had never seen him. Not cloaked in sarcasm or silence. Not sharp with fury or shuttered by guilt.

This was Alaric unbound.

When at last he slowed, the horses milling breathless about him, he turned — and saw me. He stilled — then slowly peeled away from the herd's edge, breath fogging in the air. The horses galloped on; their silhouettes lost in the thickening midday light. Alaric walking toward me now, his chest rising and falling with the remnants of exertion — steam curling from his skin, his eyes dark as the earth beneath them.

I was just as breathless. It was in that moment, even with the distance between us— I just knew, knew I was utterly, irrevocably lost to him.

"You know," he breathed, voice still rough with wind and joy, "if you were hoping to remain a mystery, you are doing a terrible job of it."

I blinked, unsure whether to laugh or scold him. "I might say the same."

"You find me at my least civilised," he said, breathless, a smirk at his lip's edge.

"I find you…" I began, and faltered. "Unexpected."

"A stalker would be more accurate," he replied lightly.

"A coincidence," I said, lifting my chin in defiance.

"And you—" he closed the distance now, eyes never leaving mine, "—you find yourself at the edge of the wood, again and again. Now you are at a place where no one even considers to find me."

Her mouth twisted. "Perhaps I like to wander."

"Perhaps," he said, eyes flicking downward as if to check the pulse at my throat, "you're drawn."

We stood, close now, and he glanced back at the horses and shrugged.

"They know who I am. Sometimes—I think they knew even before I did."

I looked back in response, then nodded in approval— desperate to hide the true effect the moment had on me. To clear the silence quickly, I answered the question I knew loomed in his mind.

"I was in the village," I said, finally. "With Una, my friend. We were cornered by two men. It was—it was— nothing."

His jaw shifted. "And yet you're here."

"James assisted us. He brought us here, said we'd be welcome—"

His hand brushed mine, barely there.

"You are."

❖

Our arms brushed as we walked side by side, back toward the house; once, twice, again, then again, like a promise neither of us yet dared to speak.

The blanket of mist trailed behind us like an unfinished verse. Passing the stables, we rose up the stone steps beneath the grand archway. The spell of the valley not broken, merely folded away for later.

The doors opened before we reached them — not by servants, but by the house itself, or so it seemed. A warmth rolled out from within. And the scent — woodsmoke, beeswax, lavender. Comfort made visible.

Inside, the floors gleamed with polish, scattered with rugs worn soft by time. Paintings lined the walls — more hands, always hands — and niches held vases brimming with cut wildflowers. There was no darkness here— only light; bouncing off one mirror, reflecting from another, illuminating any shadows that dare form.

We walked slowly, neither in haste to speak. The air held that trembling hush that often follows revelation. Each footfall over the marbled flooring felt deliberate, echoing with the weight of all that remained unsaid.

Alaric moved beside me with an ease I envied — the wildness of moments before still clung to him like a second skin. His sleeves were damp, his dark curls beginning to dry in errant waves that caught the light in glints of ebony and shadow. There was mud upon his boots, a smear of green across his cuff, and yet, in all his dishevelment, he seemed more himself than I had ever seen him.

"I suppose," I ventured at last, "that you'll expect me to believe you do this often. Run with beasts. Startle women. Shatter expectations."

His lip curled in the faintest smile. "Only on days ending in 'Y'."

I huffed a laugh despite myself. "It suits you, though. The horses. This place."

He looked sideways at me; head tilted.

"You mean more than it suits Marrowhall?"

"I mean it reveals something I hadn't yet seen." I hesitated, then added, "Something you rarely let show."

He stopped walking. I turned, finding his gaze already fixed upon me.

"This is where I am not observed," he said softly. "Where I am not a Stockholm. Where the house does not watch, and the walls do not echo with *someone else's sins*."

My chest tightened. What did that mean? Before the thought dug any deeper, I felt an intense impulse to touch him — not in passion, but in knowing, in kinship. Instead, I looked ahead.

"Thank you for having us here."

"Always".

Then, as though the moment were a candle flickering low, the air shifted. From the direction of a room at the end of the hallway, voices — soft, familiar — carried through the house. Una's lilting protest, and James's gentle drawl laced with amusement.

We walked on, now with lighter steps.

I curled around the doorframe and saw the two of them standing in the drawing room. Una's arms were crossed, her chin lifted with disobedience. James stood before her, hands raised too, showing her a stance.

"Here," he instructed. "If a man ever comes too close, you don't need strength—just aim".

He drew her arm to his neck.

"I've no need of lessons," Una muttered, though the tremor in her voice betrayed her.

"Then why do you flinch when I so much as lift my hand?"

"I don't," she snapped, eyes flashing.

James stood beside her with a rakish slant, gesturing with easy flair, as though describing some heroic battle.

"Then prove it."

She rolled her eyes.

Their dance was almost as sharp as Alaric's dance with the horses—though this was all sparks and defiance. Yet I saw it, that glint in her eye when she thought him not looking.

Una had changed into another gown — nothing too elaborate, but something much finer than her usual uniform. The dress was a soft dove-grey muslin, with a white laced high neck, matching sleeves gathered at the wrist —finished with a delicate row of buttons along the waist. It was one of many garments kept at Trewyllow for guests who might arrive unannounced — a quiet generosity; something I now sense was typical of Alaric.

On Una, it looked as though it had been made for her. The modest cut flattered her, the colour gentle against her chestnut curls, which were now half tied back with a silk ribbon I did not recognise. She moved differently, too — still measured, still composed, but with a newfound grace. As though, for the first time, the world was allowing her to take up space in it. And she did — beautifully.

I had grown accustomed to Una's composure — the careful tuck of her apron, the calm set of her features, the silence that seemed more armour than absence. She was a woman who carried herself with a stillness that others mistook for distance.

But now — here — I saw another part of her.

James again raised uncertainly as he demonstrated some defensive trick, this time with more dexterity. She laughed — truly laughed — at her own clumsiness when her footing slipped, when her hand missed its mark and landed gracelessly against his shoulder. She flushed, shook her head, and tried again. He teased her gently, and she swatted at him with more play than purpose.

Her hair had slipped loose from its pins, a rogue strand curling at her cheek. She did not notice, nor did she rush to tame it as she would have in any other company. And the sound of her laughter — unguarded, bright — startled me more than any revelation could have done.

She was no longer the maid, not the sentinel at my side, but a woman. Entirely herself.

I wanted to hold the moment in my hands, to bottle it like a rare butterfly and never let it escape. For the world would try to grind it down, would call her back into silence and shadow. But now that I had seen her as she was, I could not forget, and I would do anything to guard it — that laughter, that loosened strand of hair — from being lost again.

Deep in thought, I hadn't noticed Alaric standing beside me— close enough that his breath quivered a strand of hair clinging to my ear. His presence was a steady weight, sleeve brushing mine once more.

"He likes her,"

I blinked up at him. "And she tolerates him. For now."

Alaric let out a quiet laugh, then talking into the room, "It seems my groom has made an impression."

"Groom! —The nerve of it!" James chuckled, shaking his head in playful disapproval.

"She doesn't give in easy," I murmured back to Alaric, still clinging to the doorframe.

"No," Alaric cut in, "*But the things worth having rarely don't.*"

The words hung between us, and I glanced at him.

He wasn't looking at me, not directly. But his eyes had shifted just enough, the edges softening, his profile carved in the mellow light of the corridor. I felt something catch in my throat—a pause, a pulling— as though the space between us had shifted its weight and leaned in.

For a heartbeat, we were suspended in something unspeakable.

"If you're set on loitering, Alaric, might I request you do it quietly?" James called out from within the room, "You're interfering with a very serious lesson, and I'll not have my reputation as an instructor besmirched."

Alaric' gaze dropped, mouth twitched— a smirk or a smothered sigh, I could not tell. He stepped full into the room now, spell broke, the atmosphere returning to itself. I cleared my throat pretending I hadn't forgotten to breathe.

"A fair request." Alaric said dryly, taking his time to respond. "But do recall—James, it is I who pay you, not the other way round. I'll have you shovelling stables at dawn, as befits your *title*".

He now had a beaming grin, impressed by his whit, and cast James a look edged with humour. James rolled his eyes with exaggerated patience.

"Marrowhall's accounts will have to wait until you learn to knock."

Their exchange drew a faint smile to Una's lips. I noticed it — and so did James, who flushed slightly before returning to his posture.

As we joined them near the hearth, James turned his attention briefly to me, his voice lowering.

"He stays away from Marrowhall, you know. Too much of Edmund in the walls."

"Edmund?" I recoiled.

I felt the warmth in the room vanish. The silence thinned like mist— I turned my gaze toward Alaric. His jaw had tensed; the pleasant line of his mouth vanished beneath the bristle of something darker. But he said nothing, not a word.

It was enough.

"I think we should leave" I said, adjusting my gloves though they did not need fixing.

Una looked to me— then to Alaric—then to James.

"Yes, Miss."

James straightened; his eyes darted to Alaric— then back to me—caught in the sudden glare of what he'd unleashed.

Alaric then met my eyes.

"I'll have your carriage readied."

He didn't ask why. He didn't protest. But as he turned from me, I saw the stiffness in his shoulders. A fortress rebuilt. He stepped to the door and gently opened it. The gesture was quiet, but it rang with everything unsaid.

As I passed, he reached for my hand — not boldly, but with a startling gentleness. His fingers grazed mine, warm and bare, the faintest pressure of skin brushing skin. I looked at him— properly, wholly— his gaze met mine, steady and unreadable save for the flicker of sorrow that passed like a cloud shadowing a pool of water.

I smiled—faintly— then pulled my hand away.

His hand flexed. The breath he took was soundless, but it echoed in me as I stepped past him, across the threshold and out the door.

❖

The carriage rocked gently as it ventured back toward Penryn House. Outside, the branches tossed in the rising wind. Mist crept along the roadside; the hills swaddled in a hush of grey. Inside, I sat rigid, my gloved hands clenched in my lap. Una watched the blur of countryside but turned, at last, her voice soft.

"You love him."

I did not look away from the window.

"Don't be ridiculous."

"You do. I saw it. The way you looked at him — when you held his hand in the doorway. I've never seen anyone look at another person like that."

My jaw tightened. The truth cut through me like steel through silk. "I don't know what I feel."

"You're afraid," Una said gently. "That's all."

"Wouldn't you be?" I turned at last, eyes brimming though her voice remained steady. "After all of it? The lies, the shadows, the masks? Men who smile as they cut you? Who kiss your hand and feed you poison with the same lips?"

Una's face softened. "I never thought I'd trust again." She paused, then added, "But I trust you."

I turned away, my ache in my throat unbearable. I reached out, blindly, and took Una's hand. We said nothing more. But the silence between us was no longer emptiness. It was something forged — raw, honest, and unbreakable.

The carriage swayed as we turned from the cliffs toward the town. The road wound through the outskirts — a narrow, uneven stretch that bordered the harbour on one side and the edge of the market on the other. Stalls were half-covered now, their awnings trembling in the wind. The smell of salt and fish hung heavy in the air.

Then, the carriage lurched to a halt.

The horses snorted, stamping at the cobbles. Outside, voices rose — murmurs, then cries, the kind that ripple through a crowd before the meaning reaches you. Una leaned forward.

"What is it?"

The driver's voice came muffled through the wood. "Someone's been found, miss. Down by the water."

A chill threaded through me. I pushed open the door before reason could stop me. The wind struck cold, carrying the brine of the harbour and the sharp scent of seaweed. Ahead, a knot of townsfolk had gathered where the market road dipped toward the shore. Women in aprons, men with their sleeves rolled, children peering wide-eyed between skirts. Una followed close, her skirts catching on the damp stones as we forced our way through the throng.

And then I saw her— in the near distance.

Her body lay upon the rocks, half-shrouded in a fisherman's net, hair tangled with weed and ribbon. The sea had marked her — her skin waxen, her dress heavy with silt and sand. Then a sound rose above the surf — a woman's cry, raw and bellowing.

It wasn't a wail of shock, but of something deeper, older—ancient even — the kind of sound that lives in the bones of our ancestry. She broke through the ring of onlookers and blundered with every step. The sea lapped at her skirts, darkening them like a dabbed cloth in ink.

No one moved to stop her. No one spoke.

Her sobs carried over the rocks, rough as waves against stone. I remember thinking she sounded like the sea itself — primal, endless, pleading.

"My daughter! My beautiful girl!"

I stumbled forward, hands shaking. The woman fell to her knees beside the body, gathering the girl's head into her lap as though warmth might yet be coaxed back into her. "My beautiful girl," she kept saying, her sobs striking the air like torn cloth.

Una then crippled beside me, one hand to her mouth.

I could not breathe.

The world had narrowed to the sight of that pale face, unrecognisable yet known.

"It's her," I whispered. "Oh God, Una—it's Letty."

The name caught in my throat, breaking apart as the truth sank in. Una's hand found mine, cold and trembling. We clung to one another, sinking to the earth, both of us shuddering.

Letty's hair still shone golden auburn where the tide had not reached, tangled against the dark rocks like threads of sunlight refusing to die. That same hair I had once seen plaited neatly for work, loose and laughing in lamplight, now spread in perfect ringlets upon the shore. The sea had taken nearly everything — her colour, her breath, her song — but not that.

Around us, the villagers' voices blurred into one indistinct hum — a dirge of unease and detachment.

"Another one gone to the ocean," someone murmured.

"Pity."

Pity. The word echoed in my skull like mockery. Then, through the shifting mass of onlookers, I saw him— Lord Blackwell.

He stood apart from the crowd as though the world itself had stepped aside to make room for him. His coat was immaculate, his gloves spotless despite the mud at his feet. The air around him seemed untouched by grief, by wind, by anything human. His eyes — pale and sharp as cut glass — did not search, they assessed. He looked upon the body, upon the murmuring crowd, and I knew at once: this was not mourning. It was observation. Calculation. His gaze drifted across the faces, unhurried, unfeeling. He turned away, and for a moment, the light caught the edge of a ring: a flash of gold against the bleak surrounding.

He did not see me — but I saw him. Beyond him loomed the cliff, jagged and dark, its sheer face clawing at the sea below. And there, rising above it, stood Marrowhall — ghostly against the mist, watching from above like a beacon of war.

And in that instant, the world seemed to tilt. Marrowhall, the brothel, the smeared lipstick flashing faintly in my memory. I saw it all — the men in their velvet coats, their careless hands, their wine-dark sins. The way they smiled as though consequence were beneath them, as though girls like her were made to be bent, broken then discarded.

The sea crashed beyond, cold and relentless, and I felt its fury echo in my chest. Grief struck first — sharp, blinding — but what rose after was stronger.

It was purpose. It was wrath.

I took one last look at Letty's still, distended face; the girl who had giggled like no one was watching, a girl who whispered of dreams and fear in the same breath.

Una's sobs broke softly beside me, her head bowed. I laid a hand over hers, and when I looked toward the horizon, I did not see the sea; I saw the men who made graves of girls, lined across the skyline, one by one. I then swore to myself — in the hush between the wind, the tide and the sky that they would truly answer for this.

They would not bury her story.

They would not silence her name — Not this time.

Chapter Twenty-One

The house was too quiet. A silence hung in Penryn's halls that night — not the peaceful hush of rest, but something weighted, oppressive, like the breath of a wolf circling unseen. My steps echoed on the wooden floors; each creak too sharp, too loud. Somewhere beyond the windowpanes the storm gathered, its low growl swelling closer with every hour.

We had returned before dusk. The coach wheels still seemed to thunder in my skull, though the road was long behind us. Una's face had gone pale as driftwood, her eyes rimmed red. We hadn't spoken since the harbour, but when the house came into view, she pressed my hand and whispered, "Say nothing — not yet. They would twist it. We'll find the truth together."

And so I had nodded. But the silence she begged for burned through me like fever. Now, wandering the corridor alone, I could still see Letty's lifeless form upon the rocks — her dress torn, her hair tangled with seaweed and ribbon.

The sound of her mother's scream clung to me, raw and echoing. Every breath I drew tasted of salt and fury.

Word clearly had not reached Penryn. The lamps were lit as usual, the hearths tended, the air perfumed faintly with lavender and polish. The servants moved about with their practiced quiet, as though the world had not just broken open by the harbour. Then, from the shadows of the stairwell, I heard them — two servants I did not recognise, their voices hushed but hurried.

"Rothwell's away on business—again," one tattled, in a mocking tone.

"Better for it." the other replied.

Their voices faded into the next corridor, leaving the words to hang in the air like cobwebs. I stood still, my heart twisting strangely. A flicker of relief, quick and shameful, moved through me. His absence would grant me time — time to contemplate, to make sense of what we had witnessed, to uncover how Letty came to that shore.

This relief however, soured almost instantly. The idea of his business — his endless dealings and silences — seemed to echo with something I could not yet name. I pressed my hands to the banister, breathing hard. The silence was unbearable. I longed to shatter it — to scream, to demand, to drag the truth from wherever it hid.

Yet I knew what Una had said was right. One whisper, one misplaced word, and the truth would vanish beneath the same current that had claimed Letty.

So, I swallowed it down — the grief, the rage, the need to strike at something. The house felt colder for it. The portraits seemed to watch as I passed; the clock ticked too loudly, as though mocking my restraint. I moved down the corridor, my reflection passing darkly along the wainscot mirrors. I thought of Letty's eyes, wide and sightless, and of her mother's scream still ringing in my chest. The storm pressed harder against the glass, the wind scraping its nails along the panes. I stopped and looked toward the window, my breath catching at the sight of lightning crawling along the horizon.

The world seemed to hold its breath.

Something was coming — I could feel it, as sure as the thunder that followed. That rage, that burning desire for answers, drove me. I tried to listen to Una's instruction, and told myself I only sought distraction — a book from the library, perhaps, or some task to steady my restless hands. But my feet carried me elsewhere, down a narrow passage, into a wing I seldom entered. Toward the office.

The door yielded with a low groan. The air inside was close, heavy with the musk of leather, tobacco, and the faint bitterness of old ink. Candle stubs crowded the desk, their wax hardened into pale rivers across the wood. Books leaned in crooked towers along the shelves, their spines cracked, their titles faded. And on the desk — a stack of letters. I hesitated. To trespass here was no small thing. Yet the silence pressed me onward, the restless storm rattling at the window as though urging me to act. My hand hovered, then seized the topmost letter, its parchment worn soft with age. The handwriting struck me first: sharp, elegant strokes, every line deliberate;

My dearest Morgana,

The hour is late, and there is little left to say that will not wound you. Yet silence would be the crueller act.

Our boy, Edmund, is to be kept. Raise him gently, and let him believe what safety requires — that he was born without name or claim to the Stockholm legacy. The truth would destroy far more than it could ever redeem.

You are free now — of Marrowhall, of what lies beneath it. I will see that you are both provided for, though it must be done from afar. This is not a reflection of my love for you, but the order of the world. I am bound to it, as are you — and we must bend, lest it break us both.

Provide him with this ring, as proof of my word, and as a last trace of our love that must learn to live in silence.

With love, always,

Silas

My vision blurred. The words swam before me, striking at my heart like blows.

Edmund. Her child — a Stockholm.

Lady Hawthorne — a woman once bound, once captive in that place, the mistress, Edmund's *mother*. She was a pawn in the hands of Marrowhall and compelled to silence.

I staggered back, clutching the letter as if it burned. At its bottom, pressed into the parchment in red wax, lay a mark. Within it was embedded a ring's imprint, deep and sure — a ring I knew too well. The world tilted. The memory surged like blood from a wound: a hand seizing me before I fell to my near death, its band cold against my skin.

That ring—Edmund's ring, all along. A cry broke from my throat, low and ragged. I sank to the floor, the letter crumpling in my grasp, my body trembling as though the very foundations of the house betrayed me. It was then that I heard her. A soft step, the faint sweep of skirts. Lady Hawthorne stood in the doorway, her face pale, her eyes dark with knowledge long withheld.

"You knew," I whispered, my voice hoarse, scarcely my own. "Edmund." My breath caught. "He is your son."

She closed her eyes, and in that silence her stillness condemned her.

"Why?" My cry rose with the force of the storm outside.

"Why did you never tell me? Why let me believe him noble, when all along he was bred in shadows, and you—" My voice faltered, breaking into sobs. "You had just as much part in this."

Her lips trembled. At last, she spoke — each word torn from some deep cavern of pain.

"Because I could not bear it. To see him as he is — to watch him walk the same path — to confess that he was born of a love I could never disclose." Her voice cracked, and she turned her face away.

"I have lived each day with chains you cannot see. To speak was to shatter them upon us both. For hell to break loose." I rose unsteadily to my feet, my hands shaking, my chest burning with disbelief.

"You call this survival? Silence? Submission?"

She met my gaze then, her eyes fierce, wet, alive with old terror. "To survive as a woman, you must learn to hide, to endure, and to do what is expected of you. That is the only way the world allows us breath. Defy it, and it will devour you whole."

"I will not live caged by it," I said, my voice low, trembling.

"Then you will not live long," she answered sharply. "I have seen what happens to women who stand too tall. They are plucked down, humiliated, broken — their names dragged through mud until not even their graves are spared."

Her voice softened, almost pleading. "Edmund's temper may be unkind, but it is a man's nature to be fierce. It is in them to protect, to provide, to claim. You mistake passion for cruelty."

I shook my head, tears streaking hot across my cheeks. "You call it protection? Tell that to Letty — the girl, living under *your roof*, pulled lifeless from the sea because no one would protect her. Because men like Edmund believe they can take what they please and bury what's left."

Lady Hawthorne flinched as if struck. "Do not speak to me of that girl. I have no part in her misfortunes."

"You have part in all of it," I said, voice breaking. "Your silence feeds it. You protect the men who destroy us and call it survival."

Her composure cracked then — a sob, half-swallowed, half-spat.

"You know nothing of what it means to be a woman alone in this world. I was not always a Lady of this house— I was Morgana. And I was loved, child — loved and provided for by a man who saw my worth. He gave me safety, a name, a fortune. He saved me."

I stared at her. "He bought you."

Her breath hitched; her mouth opened, closed again. "He gave me what the world would not — peace, respect."

I stepped closer, trembling with fury.

"Respect? Respect cannot be bought, nor bound, nor sealed with rings."

Her eyes widened —but her mouth stayed shut.

"You may have been saved, Lady Hawthorne," I said softly, "but I mean to be free."

The thunder cracked outside, splitting the air. Between us, the candle flame trembled, throwing our shadows long and trembling across the walls.

"I will bring it all to light," I said, voice steady now, hollow with conviction. "Every lie. Every name. Letty will not be buried in silence."

Her expression hardened, sorrow folding into fear.

"You will ruin yourself."

"Then let ruin be the price," I whispered.

For a long moment neither of us spoke. The storm beat against the windows, the room shuddering under its weight. Then, at last, Lady Hawthorne turned away, her face pale as wax.

"Then may God have mercy on you, *Alexandra*," she said quietly. "Because the world will not."

The storm broke once more, thunder crashing so near it seemed to split the very heavens. I rose, clutching the letter and its dreadful seal, my tears mingling with the rain that drove through the shutters. She reached for me, but I recoiled. My skirts swept the floor as I fled from that chamber, the letter still clutched in my hand, the truth now carved into my very flesh. The wolf had been in my house all along. My breath came sharp, ragged.

I could not remain. Not here. Not now. My footsteps rang down the corridors, swift, frantic, as though the house itself pursued me. At the stables, my mare stamped and tossed her head against the storm, but I mounted with desperate resolve. The rain struck like needles, soaking my gown to my skin, plastering curls across my face. Mud spattered my skirts as hooves churned the sodden earth. The wind tore at me, wild and merciless, but I rode harder still. There was only one destination.

Marrowhall—for answers.

Chapter Twenty-Two

Back when the moon shone bright over Hawkstone Manor, the carriage door slammed behind Edmund with such force that the horse trembled in its traces. His jaw locked; his breath ragged. Alex was now contained, safe, like a budgie in his cage. One thought pulsed through him, violent and consuming: return to Alaric. Confront him. Tear from him what dignity he still possessed.

The moon above — fat and merciless, its silver light drenching him as he strode across the gravel. Each step carried the heaviness of something shifting, as though the bones beneath his skin strained to break free. The shadows clung tighter, his shoulders hunched, his fists curled. By the time he reached the double doors, he moved less as a man than as a beast writhing in borrowed flesh — anger and jealousy twisting every sinew.

The doors parted. Light spilled across him, gilding his pale face, but nothing softened in him. Guests turned, their voices lilting with welcomes and greetings.

"Edmund! Returned so soon?" one called, raising a Wolf laced finger in acknowledgment. Ring glinting in the reflection of the Chandelier.

He ignored them.

Another man near the stairs lifted his glass with a smirk. "Next time, Edmund, I'll have the same lady — same mask too, if you please!"

Edmund's stride did not falter. His head didn't as much as quiver. He merely raised a single hand, halting the man mid-laugh, and walked on, silent and implacable, his silence more cutting than any retort.

"Your debts, Rothwell!" another called from the darkest corner of the room, a sharp grin cutting his face. "Best see them settled by tomorrow or you'll find yourself—"

Edmund passed without a glance, the words falling dead at his heels.

His presence was answer enough. The beast grew, swelling in him, every ignored jest a claw scratching at his insides. The crowd sensed it — the shift. Polite smiles faltered, whispers flitted in his wake, as though his true shape was beginning to bleed through the mask of manhood he wore.

And then he saw him. Alaric.

Composed, as ever, his stillness the kind that drew eyes without effort. He stood apart, but not alone — never alone. His gaze found Edmund's the instant their paths crossed, as though he had expected him. As though he had been waiting.

Edmund's breath rasped. The wolf in him snapped its chain. He closed the distance in three strides and seized Alaric by the collar. Gasps rippled through the onlookers.

But Alaric — damn him — did not flinch. His hand rose calmly, prying Edmund's grip with quiet strength. He could have crushed him, Edmund knew; Alaric was the stronger. Yet he chose restraint, composure, the moral high ground that cut deeper than any blow.

"Not here," Alaric said, low but firm.

They moved, wordless, into a side chamber. The door shut behind them, muffling the music, the laughter, the world. Silence pressed in, broken only by Edmund's ragged breathing.

"You think me blind?" Edmund hissed. His mask had slipped askew, his eyes wild, bloodshot. "You think I did not see how you looked at her? How she looked at you?"

Alaric's gaze did not waver. "You mistake courtesy for—"

"Courtesy?" Edmund spat, the word breaking like glass. "How far you chose her, *brother?*"

The word hung in the air like a blow. "How far before she learns the truth of you — of us?"

Edmund stepped closer, his voice breaking into a growl. "Do you know what it is to be the bastard? The underdog? The shadow on the family tree? You — the legitimate one, the heir, the golden son. And me? The mistake. The stain. The one who gets chosen last, who does not get the name, who will never belong."

Alaric's silence was knife-sharp, but his jaw tightened.

"You think she would choose you if she knew?" Edmund's laughter was hollow, fractured. "If she knew that you — you — killed your own mother and father? That the blood of a sadistic murderer runs in your veins, as cleanly as it runs in mine?"

The words struck, hard and deliberate. Edmund watched him closely, eyes glittering.

"And do not think to forget," Edmund went on, voice lower now, colder, "that I owe men more than I can pay. That the brothel must be fed — fed with flesh and coin and —blood. I have debts, yes. But I have power too, brother. Power enough to take her from you. To ruin her. To ruin you."

Alaric's hand tightened at his side. His voice, when it came, was measured steel. "I want no part in your dealings. No part in you."

Edmund's smile twisted, all teeth— "Oh so you're still clinging to your virtue, Stockholm?" His voice low, sharp as broken glass. "You parade yourself as if the family name were unsullied. But I know the truth, no —*we* know the truth. Father's mines are nothing but graveyards now, shafts—drowned, cottages—empty, the men? Gone to Africa, Australia and God knows elsewhere. When there was no tin left to bleed, he found other veins to cut. And he left that to me."

A pause, heavy, before Edmund's laugh rang out—quiet, cruel.

"Flesh, Alaric", in a mocking tone— "Trafficked through the harbours at night, smuggled as easy as brandy. That's what keeps those walls standing firm. And you—poor, noble Alaric— you still live within them. You eat the bread, drink *my* wine." His finger slamming to his chest like a dart on a bullseye.

"Morally better, perhaps, but chained to the same ruin. Bonded by the same blood!"

Edmund pulled a small blade from his pocket, then carved it into his palm. His blood spilled, emptying into a neighbouring whiskey glass, which laid perfectly on the side table. He then raised the glass, as if to toast to a bountiful feast,

"You go down with us too brother, whether you like it or not. You may not wear the ring, but our seal is scorched on your soul." His fist pounded his chest, as a virile ape would claiming his territory.

"—So I kindly request", he slammed the glass onto the drawing table next to them, "—Keep away from her. Leave her to me, or by God—" He leaned in, his breath hot, the beast fully bared. "I will make you regret it."

The silence that followed was terrible, the air taut as a drawn bow. The wolf in him trembled on the edge of breaking free.

Alaric remained composed; no words left his mouth—no emotion summoned on his face. Not a draw of breath was out of line, too long, or too short—not even one twitch of his eye as he knew all too well that any reaction would give Edmund satisfaction —He would give not one inch of it.

Silence lingered on.

And then suddenly, with a violent jerk of his coat, Edmund turned. The door rattled as he wrenched it open, his steps striking the marble like blows. The music of the soirée spilled back into him, a parody of gaiety, but he did not slow. As he moved through the ballroom, his wound wept freely, thin rivulets marked his path across the marble. He did not seem to notice—nor care.

The crowd drew back, careful not to step in what he left behind. The droplets glimmered darkly in the candlelight—small, perfect reminders of all the unseen blood his hands had already shed. He passed among them like a man absolved, every stain disguised as ceremony.

The main doors then opened in haste, and the night met him— cold and unsparing. His stride smoothed, the fury folding cleverly in upon itself. His hands—now gloved once more, ring and wound—wrapped and concealed.

The carriage awaited him, black and gleaming, the horses restless. As he approached, a figure detached itself from the darkness — his footman, hat lowered, coat collar turned high. He bowed slightly; his voice pitched low enough to vanish beneath the hum of the storm.

"The girl has been taken care of, sir."

Something small glinted in the man's palm. He held it out. A locket.

A simple trinket, dull with salt and soil, yet its hinge still streaked with a girl's desperate touch. It swung once from its chain before falling into Edmund's palm. For a heartbeat, neither spoke. The weight of the thing was light — far too light for what it meant.

Edmund turned it over once, his thumb tracing the worn edge, the faint engraving barely visible in the dark. Then, with a calmness that might have been mistaken for indifference, he closed his fist around it.

"Very well," he said softly and slipped swiftly it into his pocket. For a moment before he entered, he paused. In the window's sheen he saw himself reflected — no beast, no brother's shadow, no illegitimate wretch, but a man again. The *perfect* gentleman.

He plucked a stray hair from his coat sleeve, smoothed the fabric with fastidious care, and reached for the carriage door.

Chapter Twenty-Three

The gallery loomed before me like a sentinel of stone, its black windows gleaming with the storm's reflection. Rain lashed the courtyard, hissing against flagstones, while the sea's roar carried inland on the wind. My mare stamped and tossed her head, foam at her bridle, but I barely felt her movements beneath me — I rode as though possessed, driven by revelation and terror.

When I reached the steps, I flung myself down, skirts heavy with rain, hair whipping my face in tangled ropes. My hand still clenched the crumpled letter, the seal's broken wax bleeding into my palm. I pounded upon the oak doors with a fist that trembled as much with fury as with cold.

No answer.

Only the groan of timbers, the howl of the gale. I pressed forward regardless, the door yielding to my desperate shove. Inside, the air was cool and stale, carrying the faint tang of linseed oil and dust. Shadows stretched like wounds across the floor, broken by the erratic flash of lightning from the tall windows. And there — at the far end of the hall, draped in gloom — the painting.

The same painting that had held me the night I first encountered him. The carriage, its wheels rearing over the abyss. The horses, wide-eyed with terror. The fall frozen in an eternal instant, all motion suspended but for the horror on the figures' faces — man and woman, clinging to each other, their doom written in every brushstroke.

I stepped closer, my breath ragged. The storm outside illuminated it in savage bursts, each detail flaring into stark relief. My eyes stung, my throat burned.

"It was you," I whispered. "Alaric—it was your hand that painted this."

The crack of the door behind me jolted my heart into my throat. I turned — and there he stood.

Rain streaked his dark hair, his coat hung sodden, his boots tracked mud across the marble. His chest heaved with the effort of haste; his gaze fixed upon me with an intensity that seemed to cut through the darkness. Alaric Stockholm, unmasked, unguarded.

"You should not be here," he said hoarsely, though his voice betrayed no anger — only strain, raw as the storm itself. "Not tonight."

"Then tell me why," I cried, thrusting the letter forward, my hand shaking. "Tell me why I found this — why I see torment on these walls — why you have let me walk blind while Edmund poisons everything around us!"

Lightning cleaved the sky, flooding the chamber with white fire. "Or are you indeed cut from the very same cloth? Have I been a fool all along to—to dance with the devil. You have beguiled me, against my will —Does it satisfy you to see my soul bled dry?".

In an instant his face was laid bare — anguish carved deep as if by a sculptor's hand. He approached, slow, deliberate, as though nearing a creature half-wild. His eyes flicked to the letter in my grasp, then back to my face.

"You read it." he murmured. Not a question—an acknowledgement. "Then you know."

155

"I know enough!" I cried, my voice breaking, "to see that everything has been lies. Edmund—his birth, his shadows, the brothel—" My throat closed on the word. I was spiralling into the abyss.

"And you—you painted this. Why not tell me—Why conceal it?"

He stopped mere steps away, his wet hair clinging to his brow, his hand half-lifted as though to touch me, though he did not dare. "Because it is my burden. Not yours."

"Not mine?" The cry tore from me. "How dare you say so, when it has become mine whether I will it or not! When his hand—" I faltered, my breath catching. "When his hand nearly ended me, Alaric — I was that girl that flung herself from the window that day. Tabitha. Tabitha Redfern. He killed her—Killed me."

His jaw tightened. His eyes — dark, furious, haunted — did not leave mine. "It was Edmund?"

The words, spoken aloud, cracked the air like thunder. A truth too long withheld, now forced into sound.

"Yes," I whispered. "It was Edmund. I know now. But what of you? You must have known —must have let it happen? You said nothing—"

"—I could not," he cut in, his voice rough as gravel. "He holds me with chains you cannot see! My father's sins, mother and father's deaths, Crimea — all of it bound around my throat like a noose. That painting—" He gestured, his hand trembling. "It is the only confession I have ever dared make."

My heart pounded. "You blame yourself."

"I was a boy," he said, his tone raw, stripped bare. "A boy who should have seen, who should have stopped them. I watched the wheels break, the horses bolt, the cliff give way. I stood helpless as they fell — and since that hour I have been nothing but the echo of that moment."

My anger ceased— the truth settled upon me.

"And Edmund, my brother—" His breath shuddered.

Brother— Of course.

My legs trembled at the confession.

"He knows my agony. He reminds me. He twists the guilt like a blade in my side, until I cannot draw breath without hearing it."

The storm raged beyond the glass, thunder booming like cannon-fire. My tears mingled with the rain on my skin, hot against cold. I could not speak for the ache in my chest.

At last, his composure cracked. He stepped closer, so close the warmth of him pierced the damp chill, his eyes burning into mine with a force that left me trembling.

"But you," he said, low, almost broken, "since the gallery, since the first moment you looked upon that painting— Alexandra, you are the only thing that has made me believe I might yet live. That I might yet be more than a shadow of pure grief and sorrow."

His hand rose — bare, trembling — and brushed the wet curls from my cheek, just as he did that morning by the sycamore. My breath stammered, caught between ribs that felt too tight for air. The world felt heavy—

"I should not say it," he whispered, his lips so near my ear I felt the ghost of them. My head swam.

"You are my reckoning and my refuge; to you I have bound my heart, for life or ruin." The words crashed over me heavier than thunder, more shattering than lightning. My heart lurched, my breath ragged. For a moment, we were the storm itself, raw and uncontainable.

—Then suddenly, the sound dropped away. My knees buckled; the floor rushed up. My body folded in on itself, weightless, boneless. There was no breath left to hold. Just the dizzy, spiralling sense of being completely undone.

Then — black.

Chapter Twenty-Four

I awoke as though surfacing from a dream not wholly my own. For a moment, I did not know where I lay. The light was soft, pearled through gauze curtains that shifted faintly in the sea-breeze. The steady rhythm of the storm had faded in the night, leaving only the hush of waves breaking distantly upon the land.

My body was heavy, yet unexpectedly at peace. The ache in my limbs seemed eased, my heart less frantic than when I had fled last night. And then I felt it — the warmth at my side.

He had not left me. His arm, strong yet forgiving, curved gently around my waist as though guarding me even in sleep. His breath was slow, steady, brushing the hair at my temple. I lay still, listening to it, scarcely daring to move lest the spell shatter.

The letter, the gallery, the storm — all of it hovered at the edge of memory like phantoms at a windowpane. Yet here, in this hush, I felt another truth: that I had been carried, not abandoned; that in my weakness I had been rescued, not condemned.

Carefully, I turned, and my gaze fell upon him. The storm had carved itself into his features: the dark smudges beneath his eyes, the unshaven line of his jaw, the restless furrow of his brow even in repose. Yet there was a boyishness there too — a fragile peace that stole upon his face when sleep released him from guilt's relentless grip.

My fingers itched to touch him. I resisted — but only for a moment. Then, like a thief, I let them graze the curl of hair that fell against his cheek. He stirred faintly, his lips parting, but he did not wake.

The room itself seemed to breathe with us. The fire looked as though it had long since gone out, leaving only the pale warmth of dawn. The salt air seeped through the shutters, tinged with earth and rain. I drew it in like sacrament.

But peace is never long-lived in a house haunted by wolves.

I remembered the weight of the letter still hidden within my gown; its words etched as if into my very skin. I remembered Mrs Hawthorne's confession — her silence, her treachery. And Edmund—Edmund whose presence lay like a shadow even now upon my chest.

Alaric shifted then, his arm tightening as though he sensed my unrest. His eyes opened slowly, dark and blurred by sleep. When they focused upon me, a softness entered them I had never seen before.

"Ah, you are awake," he murmured, his voice low, thick with the remnants of slumber.

I swallowed; my throat dry. "Yes."

For a heartbeat we only looked at one another, silence wrapping us in a veil as fragile as glass. Then, with a tenderness that undid me, he brushed the back of his fingers along my cheek.

"I thought you might be gone when I woke," he confessed, scarcely more than a whisper.

I shook my head, though tears pricked my eyes.

"Not yet."

He studied me as though those words bore all the weight of eternity. And then he pressed his brow to mine, closing his eyes as if in prayer.

"The cold had got to you; I carried you here to rest—You are welcome to stay as long as you need".

"Thank you." I whispered, and planted a kiss on his forehead—an exchange that felt as natural as the turning of the Earth itself.

The air was thick, full of unanswered questions, unspoken feelings. My dress still laid upon me, perfectly untouched, although slightly damp. His coat hung discarded over a chair; his boots left in disorder by the door. And yet he remained in his shirt, cravat abandoned and his dark hair falling in careless waves across his brow.

We remained facing one another. Neither spoke, neither moved — only the dim hush of morning wrapped us, broken by the soft patter of rain against the windows and the far-off cry of gulls. His eyes held mine as though the night had left us bound in some secret tether.

I could not look away. His gaze was unflinching, dark yet strangely gentle, the kind that stripped away every veil until I felt laid bare before him. My hand rested between us on the coverlet, trembling faintly, though I fought to still it. He did not touch me, yet the nearness of him — the heat of his breath, the rise and fall of his chest — was a torment almost unbearable.

He drew a breath, slow and deliberate, his hand lifting an inch from the coverlet before he stilled it, restraining himself. "Alex, what passed last night—"

"—was more than I can yet comprehend," I broke in, my voice trembling. "And it terrifies me."

His brow furrowed, his gaze sharpening. "Terrifies you?"

"I fear myself," I whispered. "I fear what I feel when I am near you. I—I was raised to distrust desire. And yet—" My breath caught. "And yet, lying here, I cannot but feel how fragile that resolve becomes." The words broke, my courage faltering.

"I know what lies beneath here, what women are kept for, what men do with them. And I cannot silence the thought — what if you are no different? What if—"

His hand closed over mine then, warm, firm, bare. His voice came low, fierce, each syllable wrought with anguish:

"Never—I have *never* touched a woman in that place. *Not once. Not ever.*"

My heart stumbled. I stared at him, uncertain whether to believe such a vow. But his gaze did not falter; it burned with a desperate honesty.

"Not once," he said again, as if to hammer the truth into me. "I could not. I would not. The very thought of it is abhorrent. My hands may be stained with paint, with gunpowder even — but never with that. I swore long ago that I would not be the brute who takes what is not freely given."

Tears pricked hot against my lashes.

"Then free them," I said suddenly, my voice shaking yet resolute. "Free those women below. If you are not the brute, if you are not complicit, then let them go. Tonight. At once."

The demand hung between us like a sword. His expression faltered, shadowed. He drew back, just slightly, his hand slipping from mine. A silence passed, heavy as stone, before he answered.

"It is not possible. Not yet."

"Not possible?" The words tore from me, sharp, incredulous. I pushed myself upright, the sheets falling loose about me. "You speak as if they were pawns on a board, as if lives may be bartered or delayed! They are women — flesh and blood, not ghosts for Edmund's chains. Do you not see that every moment they remain there is another wound carved into them?"

His jaw tightened.

"Do you think I do not know?" His voice was low, shaking with anger he tried to master. "Do you think I do not hear them in my dreams, see them in every shadow of this house? But if I act rashly, if I strike before I have the means, Edmund will tighten his grasp, and they will suffer more. He holds power you do not yet understand."

"That is no answer," I cried, my throat raw. "You make yourself gaoler by your silence. What am I to believe, Alaric?"

I swung my legs from the bed, trembling as I gathered myself. "If you will not save them, then I cannot stay. I cannot lie here warm while they are imprisoned below."

"Alex——"

I turned from him, my fingers shaking as I fastened the bodice. But before I could take another step, his hands caught mine. Bare hands — warm, pleading — holding me fast—without force, only with urgency.

His voice broke, rough as gravel.

"Do not go—Please. If you leave now, thinking me complicit, thinking me coward — I will never forgive myself." His forehead bent low, his breath against my knuckles.

"I swear to you, Alex, I will end it. I will bring it down brick by brick if I must. But not yet — not until I can be certain Edmund cannot strike back. Not until I can shield you as well as them."

Tears blurred my sight. "I cannot wait forever."

He lifted his gaze then, his eyes dark and fierce, the storm of the night before still smouldering there.

"Nor would I ask you to. But wait— Please — Trust me."

The fight in me trembled, faltered, and yet did not die. I drew a breath, heavy with grief.

"Then prove it. Prove you are not your brother."

His grip tightened on my hands, and he pressed them to his chest, to the wild hammer of his heart.

"I will."

Chapter Twenty-Five

Voices in the corridor carried like stray threads, careless and betrayable. I had meant them to pass me by — servants' talk was usually a rope of judgement and gossip — but that morning each syllable struck like a chime I could not ignore.

"Orders from Master Edmund," murmured one maid as she brushed past the doorway; her voice trembled in that way small mouths do when they carry too-large tales. "See to the lower rooms. Ready them for the evening. He says everything must be as the gentlemen expect."

"Everything?" another returned, with the caution of one who has learned to fold knowledge into silence.

"Provided and—arranged. He's very particular this time. He's been here since dawn—down below—sorting the girls. Wants the best masks for the guests."

The phrase lodged in me like a bone. My blood congealed. Edmund — down below. Arranging. Setting out women like spoils upon a board.

It was as if the house itself inhaled; outside, somewhere, a storm-swell growled, but within those corridors the air turned colder still.

For a long moment I stood, palms flat upon the table, the old oak biting into the flesh of my hands, thinking only of the women whose voices I had not yet heard except in the clatter and hush of rumours. How many? What had been promised them? What had they been given to wear when the gentlemen called?

A decision — sharp and terrible — pushed of its own accord into my mind.

Alaric found me before I could move, his eyes quick upon my face — reading, pleading, already a man who had learned to watch me as if I might be lost if he did not hold the line.

"They speak of his orders," I said, hardly a whisper. "He is here, arranging them. He is holding a 'masquerade' for his confidants—I assume you know what that entails." A shudder chimed down each vertebra as I spoke the words.

He closed his mouth as if to stop something that would have leapt free of him. For a heartbeat he seemed to weigh the options like coins. Then he exhaled, a hard sound.

"Stay with me," he began. "Hide in my rooms. I will not have you meet his eye." There was urgency in the command, but it carried no commanding cruelty. But I shook my head.

"No, Alaric. Hiding will not help me. If we are to fight this—if we are ever to free them—I must see it with my own eyes— see who and what is involved in this, to gut it from the inside out."

The words trembled out of me, sharper than I meant, but I could not call them back. I forced my voice gentler, the plea rising despite myself.

"Please come with me. If you stand beside me, I can bear it."

He stilled, his jaw tightened, the muscle flickering as if every instinct in him recoiled. For a long moment he did not answer; his gaze drifted past me, to the shadowed corner of the room, as though he searched for some anchor that might give him the strength to deny me.

When at last he spoke, his voice was hoarse, frayed at the edges.

"You ask me to walk you into a pit." His eyes found mine again, fierce and unflinching. "Do you know what you are asking of me? My every instinct—every part of me—cries to keep you from it. To bolt the door, to shut out the night, to lock you here where nothing can touch you." His hand twitched against the latch in his mind, as if he might yet do it. I could see the battle in him — the pull of his terror against the iron of my resolve. His words weighed heavy on my heart.

"Alaric..." My voice barely rose above a whisper.

He drew a breath, ragged, and shut his eyes as if to steady himself. When they opened again, they burned with something fierce and unyielding.

"But if you go," he said at last, rough and low, "then yes—of course I will be with you. I would follow you even into the jaws of hell itself." The admission shuddered between us, fragile and irrevocable, as though he had surrendered not only to my request but to something deeper that he could no longer deny.

He set a hand to the door's latch, pressing it down, listening for the click. The sound was soft, deliberate — the sort of sound one remembers when the world is full of louder things. He turned then, crossing the room in long, purposeful strides, checking other passages, the window, the faint seam of light beneath the sill.

I looked around — the low fire guttering in the grate, the dusted sheen of books, canvases leant against the wall, the faint scent of woodsmoke, dried paint and something older still. The air itself seemed shaped by him: steady, exacting, yet full of that strange, solemn warmth I had come to know. It felt as though the room were an extension of the man — strong lines, dark corners, a sense of order barely containing its pulse.

"You must change," he said without preamble. "You cannot be seen as Alexandra tonight. Edmund will notice

165

you instantly. I will fetch you something to wear." He hesitated, searching my face. "And a mask."

"Will the mask not merely betray me in another way?" I asked. The thought of wearing one while women below wore none tasted of charades I did not wish to play.

"It will not betray you to those who wish you harm," Alaric answered. "It will hide your face; it will give us time. I will be back before the dusk swallows the light."

He left me then, and the hush of his absence folded over the room like velvet. I stood between canvases that carried storms and faces, and the very colours themselves seemed to echo the tumult in my blood.

❖

The adjoining room was dim and fragrant, the air steeped in lavender and faint traces of steam. A copper bath stood near the hearth.

I turned the tap, and water spilled out in a slow, echoing rush — the sound filling the silence like breath after grief. Steam began to rise, curling against the walls and the faint sheen of the mirror. I reached for the small glass vial upon the stand — oil of lavender — and poured a few drops into the water. They spread like pale silk across the surface, thin ribbons catching the light before vanishing. The scent deepened, heady and familiar, turning the air almost sweet.

When the bath was near full, I slipped the gown from my shoulders; the fabric fell with a clinging whisper, it peeled away from my skin until damp silk pooled at my feet. My skin prickled in the cool air before I sank into the water's warmth. It closed around me like an embrace, heavy and fragrant, laced with blossoms that floated upon the surface like small, forgiving eyes.

I let my head fall back against the rim, eyes closing as the scent wrapped around me. I could feel the salt loosen in my hair, the grime fade from my hands, as though I were rinsing away not dirt but the weight of worry. The water lapped against me with a sound like breathing.

For a moment, I could almost forget. The world beyond the door ceased to exist; there was now only the faint hiss of the lilting fire, the low hum of the house breathing through its walls, and the rhythm of my own pulse beneath the water.

When I decided to retreat from the slumber, the escape. I dressed at last in an undressed simplicity — a clean chemise, a loose wrap that Alaric had left upon a chair — I wandered to the window. The panes were streaked with rain; beneath, the gardens lay mottled and bruised. I perched upon the sill, my toes curled in the narrow ledge, my hands pressed to the cool glass.

The gallery below had been a theatre of doom and of confession; it had become in my mind, a mirror of silence. I could not help but imagine the rooms beneath Marrowhall as they were prepared: lamps trimmed to throw flattering light, cushions set just so, the heavy perfumed scent of powder masking the iron tang of blood and sorrow.

How did it feel, I asked myself, to stand upon a platform arranged by a man who saw you as a commodity? How did it feel to have a gentleman's laughter be the curtain that fell upon your dignity? The thought of them — of their small hands smoothed, of their eyes made bright with paint so they might smile for another's pleasure — twisted my gut.

Dark imaginings followed: the hush of orders, the clack of keys, a door eased on its hinges and the cool chill of sub-basements that keep their dead and secrets. I felt the old vertigo return, that same unearthly pull that had sent me over the gallery's ledge once before. For an instant the glass before me was not glass at all but the edge of the very cliff I had thought I had left behind.

The thought of leaping rose, sudden and foolish, then fell away as quickly as it had come. I clenched my fists until my knuckles blanched, and forced the day back into its proper place.

A pounding at the door made me startle. Alaric returned, carrying in his arms a bundle of satin: a ravishing gown of cherry and complementary tones, its fabric cut to the evening and fitting my form like a glove. The satin gleamed even in the subdued light, and as he laid it out upon the bed, I felt a strange, conflicted warmth.

Beside it, the mask he had chosen was beautiful — black velvet edged with a sober braid, covering three-quarters of the face; it would hide me among the crowd yet still, in a face-to-face meeting, risk recognition. That must be avoided at all costs. Fortunately, Edmund was not expecting me' perhaps, with this guise, I might just pull it off.

"You may pass as one of them yet," he uttered.

A smile rose unbidden, only to quickly die upon my lips, as a cold realisation took hold: the dawn we had awoken to this morning was nothing but a pause, a breath before the true tempest.

❖

With careful fingers I gathered my hair, securing it with the jet combs I already had from the previous day. The way my hair was placed was not extravagant—deliberately so—but there was still a quiet romance in the way some curls slipped free to brush against my throat, another softening the line of my cheek. Even in simplicity, I longed—perhaps foolishly—for him to notice.

The gown fit as though it had been made for me, cinching at the waist and flowing in a way that made my figure defiant beneath the heavy fabric. I pressed the mask to my face; its velvet was cool and slightly prickly against my cheek. When I met my own reflection, the woman staring back felt like a stranger; the high crimson of my cheeks concealed, my eyes darkened to black, hands hidden in long sleeves.

The air stirred behind me, a quiet shift; My gaze lifted to the mirror's edge—And he was there.

Alaric stood in the archway, half claimed by shadow, his silhouette merging with the darkness so fully he might have been carved from it. His eyes found me in the mirror's glass, steady and piercing, carrying both a reverence and a restraint that made my breath falter.

In that half-light, he seemed almost otherworldly. His dark hair, thick and unruly, caught the lamplight in bronze glints, as though no brush or finger had ever quite tamed it. Even with distance, his eyes — a startling grey, like slate cliffs before a storm — did not release me. He wore a full suit cut in sharp fashion; with a pitch-black fabric precise upon his frame, sleek as sin, which caught the light like rain drops and drank it in. It was paired deliciously with a waistcoat of deep burgundy paisley, rich like the finest wine and intricate as though he carried some secret rebellion in colour. A fine chain looped from his pocket to a watch of curious make, one he had once told me did not merely tell the hour, but mapped the turn of the world itself — the rising and setting of suns beyond our own. It suited him: bound not only to the earth but also beyond.

When he moved, there was no hesitation, only the quiet confidence of someone accustomed to shadowed corners and the silence between heartbeats. His gestures were unhurried, deliberate, like a painter setting each stroke with care. Even in urgency, there was grace — the kind that belongs to those who carry too much weight, but refuse to let it bend them.

He stood before the elongated mirror, which stood opposite to mine, drawing the mask over his face with deliberate care. Black velvet — soft as breath, dark as midnight — moulded to his skin as though made for him alone. It curved along the cut of his cheekbones, the fine slope of his nose, the line of his mouth— until the man before me seemed made of only shadow and breath.

It did not hide him. It defined him.

His hair now fell untamed across his brow, a loose strand brushing the edge of the mask. He pushed it back absently, the movement slow, unhurried, completely unaware that it carried the weight of every thought I shouldn't be having.

I told myself to look away. I did not.

Something primal stirred beneath my ribs — not fear, but a deep yearning. The kind that draws the tide to the moon, the flame to its wick. I felt heat rise along my throat, the hairs on the back of my spine arousing.

Still stood before the mirror, he began fastening the mask with slow precision. The lamplight played across his throat where the collar of his shirt had come undone, the faintest glint of skin visible. He turned ever so slightly, catching my reflection behind him, eyes once again finding mine in his mirror; it was a reflection upon reflection—an infinite enclosure of longing.

"Alex, would you—" his voice low, velvet roughened at the edges. He gestured to the untamed ribbon at the back of his neck.

For a moment I didn't move. Then I did. The distance between us closed too quickly, and I caught the faint scent of him — cedar, smoke, something deeper I couldn't fathom, let alone even name. The ribbon was warm beneath my fingers, and tickled every ridge on my fingertips as it glided across. My hands brushed the back of his collar, grazing the base of his neck.

He stilled.

"Here?" I whispered.

He inclined his head, not looking at me, though his voice came quieter now, taut as wire. "Tighter—please."

The words were barely sound — more breath than command — but it unravelled something deep within me.

I pulled the ribbon firm, the movement small, almost chaste. But the silence that followed was not.

He met my eyes in the mirror again. No smile, no courtesy, no mask of civility. Just the kind of look that finds its mark and stays there. The look that burns, etches, torments. And though neither of us moved, the air felt alive — thick with the ache of things that could not, must not, be spoken.

The knot sat perfectly now, dark against the white of his collar. I took half a step back, heart racing; meaning to reclaim the air between us, to remember myself — but the room had grown smaller, thick with breath and heat and something I dared not name. The flame in the lamp fluttered, throwing our reflections across the mirror like ghosts that would not part.

Then— the back of his finger laced my leg, a featherlight pressure, which felt more like breath than touch, slowly glided in an upward, gentle motion. The touch sent a shiver through me, like a whisper against the spine.

My body reacted.

He released. The movement was deliberate, quiet, as if to prove that he could. I thought — foolishly, recklessly — that I might forget to breathe. I slipped the back of my earring with unsteady hands, desperate to find something to occupy them.

"We'll be late," I said, though my voice didn't sound like my own. He smiled — that half-curve of the mouth that never reached his eyes, yet warmed the air between us all the same.

"Then let us make them wait."

His words struck through me; my knees almost buckled from the impact. I turned to fetch my gloves from the chair, telling myself more air would settle if I simply moved further. The silk lay waiting, pale as moonlight, and I reached for it — but before my fingers could close, his hand found mine. Not forcefully. Just there. Warm, steady, deliberate.

"Alex—"

My name in his voice was a slow ache, the faintest rasp at the edge of control, yet it unmade me all the same. The space around us seemed to hush, as if the very air had drawn in its breath. I turned my face toward his, where I found his eyes, half-hidden behind the mask. They were steady, dark, consuming.

"Yes?" I meant to whisper in response. But the word died in my throat. The faint lamplight caught the curve of his cheek, the hollow beneath his jaw where a pulse stirred. I felt it as though it were my own. His eyes still held mine, still burning, the mask turning them darker, deeper, almost obsidian.

He took another step closer— one deliberate movement that brought us so near our reflections blurred into one. I felt the heat of him, the faint brush of his sleeve against my arm.

My will faltered.

Then his hand left mine. It rose slowly, tracing the air until his fingers found the nape of my neck. The contact was feather-light — a whisper of warmth against skin — yet it sent a shiver clear to my heart. His palm lingered there, guiding rather than commanding, as if he could lead me without ever moving at all. Our foreheads nearly touched. I could feel the tremor of his breath, the faintest quiver where control warred with desire.

The ribbon of his mask hung loose against his collar, and I saw how the faintest tremor ran through his jaw, how his breath faltered as his gaze dropped to my mouth. The silence grew unbearable, the distance between us thinned to a single heartbeat.

His thumb brushed once against the edge of my jaw, and my lips parted — a question, a surrender, I could not tell which. The world felt suspended; time itself seemed to hold us aloft on a precipice. we hovered on the edge of it — the fall, the surrender—

—Then a sound shattered the stillness.

Hooves on gravel. Laughter echoing down the drive. The sharp rattle of a carriage wheel striking stone. He drew in a breath, straightened, and turned toward the window. The movement was swift, instinctive — the retreat of a man who has lived too long beneath watchful eyes.

"They're arriving," he said quietly. His voice was measured again, though the pulse in his throat betrayed him.

I nodded, though the motion felt like a lie. The moment had vanished, scattered like ash. Only its warmth remained, burning low beneath my skin. How easily I could have ran toward him now, how fiercely I longed to fully surrender to him. But the weight of duty now pressed against that desire.

The energy between us shifted as he turned back to me, the mask casting his face half in shadow.

"You will be safe with me," he reassured. "And if anything moves wrong — if Edmund's shadow creeps too close — you must slip away. I have set means. There are passages in Marrowhall that are not known to the staff; I will show them to you if the time comes."

"Passages?" I echoed, thinking of secrets made literal in stone and brick. "Would you lead me through them as if I were contraband?"

"As if you were the earth itself," he answered with a grim softness. "Because you are more than coin or mask. Because you are not for sale— nor ever will be."

His words struck through me, stilling the tremor beneath my ribs. They were not flattery, but faith — raw, undeserved faith — and it shook me more than fear ever could. The sight of his eyes, the warmth of his presence in mine, gave my fear a purpose.

I would be there tonight, not to admire the tapestries nor the gilded chandeliers, but to see, to note, to remember faces and names. If there was a way to save them, to expose the rot, I would find it with him by my side.

We stood for a breath — two souls attired in uncertain armour, between canvas and window, the noise of servants like the prelude to some ominous play beyond the door.

"Ready?" Alaric asked finally, stepping forward.

He offered his arm with the formality of a gentleman, yet the gesture was more than courtesy. In his composure I felt the strain of a man holding himself too tightly, as though one slip might reveal all he fought to conceal.

I pulled my mask down an inch, peered into his eyes as if asking for a last confession. Then, without warning, he drew me close and pressed his lips hard to the centre of my forehead.

It was not a tender kiss, but a claiming one — fierce in its stillness, final in its grace. A soldier's vow before the field, a man's silent confession when words would fail. The warmth of it burned through me long after he withdrew, leaving the faintest ache — as though he had placed a part of himself there, should he never return to claim it.

"You must look nothing but a stranger Alex. Speak little—move as though you belong nowhere and everywhere."

I clung to each word.

As we walked through the hallway, arm in arm, I peered through the tall windows of the hall — the sky was bruised and waiting, a wounded violet fading into dusk. Below, the drive had come alive with arrivals. Carriages lurched through the evening mist like beasts burdened with finery, their lamps throwing crooked halos against the gravel. Servants rushed to and fro, their movements brisk, rehearsed, almost desperate. Guests emerged one by one — faces already hidden, laughter spilling too loudly into the night. Jewels flared at throats and wrists, masks gleamed pale as bone. The sound of it all — silk dragging, hooves striking stone, the brittle chatter of pleasure — carried the false brightness of a theatre about to descend into tragedy.

Tonight, in velvet and shadow, the wolves would come to hunt. We would meet them on their own field, and something in me; outrage, righteousness, perhaps a madness born of grief — would not let me turn away.

Justice.

Justice for the nameless and the silenced. For the girls who were promised safety and found only ruin.

For Letty, whose small hands had reached for mercy and met the sea.

For Tabitha, who was swallowed whole by the men who thought themselves gods.

For every woman taught to lower her eyes, close her ears and endure.

If this night was to burn, then let it burn bright enough to light every shadow they had built — and may its ashes mark where I refused to bow.

Chapter Twenty-Six

The gallery's staircase stretched before me like a stage, and I its reluctant actress. My arm rested among Alaric's, trembling faintly though his grip was steady, sure, as though he alone could tether me against the storm within.

The silk of my gown whispered with every cautious step — cherry-hued, rich as blood spilled in candlelight, lined with subtle tones that shifted as I moved. Upon my face, the mask pressed close, its intricate design both shield and prison. It concealed three-quarters of me, yet I feared it exposed enough that Edmund's gaze might pierce through, if ever it found me.

The scene below glittered with extravagance: chandeliers dripping crystal like frozen tears, a thousand candles mirrored in gilt frames and glass, gowns and feathers and jewels set ablaze by their glow. Perfume and cigar smoke mingled in the air until it grew cloying, suffocating. The floor shone so bright that dancers appeared to glide upon it like restless spirits.

Then, the ballroom stirred. Conversations faltered, laughter ceased, and one by one, heads lifted. All eyes rose toward us. They did not look at me, though my cheeks burned with the scrutiny. No — it was him. It was Alaric.

He, who had never joined Edmund's gaudy revelries, who had haunted the solitude of the gallery while others drank and danced, now stood above with a lady on his arm. The sight of him struck them all silent, struck me too, as if I walked in some impossible dream. The whispers spread swift as fire through the crowd.

I felt the weight of their stares, raking across me. Who was I, they wondered, to stand at Alaric's side? I dared not answer even within myself.

"Steady," Alaric murmured low, his breath brushing my temple — a whisper meant for me alone. His hand pressed firm at the small of my back, guiding me forward as the stairwell unfolded beneath us, pale marble gleaming like ice in the candlelight.

As we began to descend, the hall opened wide, vast and glittering, every chandelier blazing with false stars. The music, unaware of our presence, swelled from somewhere unseen — violins weaving through laughter that rang too high, too brittle. Masks still turned upward, faces half-lit, half-lost. Every face was a creature, every gaze a prayer to some forgotten god — rams and wolves, stags and swans, the old myths made flesh beneath the chandeliers. I felt their gaze climb toward me, felt the weight of curiosity sharpen into hunger.

Alaric moved beside me with quiet certainty, his presence a steady flame amid the glare. My hand rested lightly upon his arm; to tighten would be to betray myself. I counted each step as though they might splinter beneath me, each breath timed to the rhythm of the music below. Not one foot could go wrong. Not even a loose curl could falter. Here, grace was in fact armour, and silence, survival.

When we reached the marble floor at last, the crowd seemed to part, slow and serpentine, making room not for guests, but for prey. The air was thick with perfume and laughter, with the scraping of violins that seemed too shrill, too bright, as though mocking the shadows that clung in the corners.

I moved among them, half-lost in a sea of silks, when something caught the light — a glint at a man's hand as he raised his glass. A ring: heavy, silver, set with the carving of a familiar wolf's head, its jaws frozen in a perpetual snarl. I noticed the same rings glinting at the dice table, at the far end of the gallery, upon the balustrade where gentlemen leaned to watch the dancers below — everywhere the beast gleamed.

My breath caught. I saw the rings flash like small moons with every gesture, every lifted goblet, every flick of the wrist. It was not fashion, not chance—It was allegiance. A brotherhood unmasked, though each face remained hidden. In that instant, the music no longer sounded like merriment; it sounded like a chant.

And then the doors opened. A hush fell—heavier, darker. Edmund had been summoned.

He emerged wreathed in cigar smoke, its grey coils curling about him like some unholy veil. A woman clung to each arm, painted smiles frozen on their lips, their gowns scandalously cut, as if to flaunt their degradation.

Edmund's mask was fashioned from black feathers, each one lacquered to a subtle sheen, their tips glinting like obsidian under candlelight. A sharp beak extended from the bridge, catching the gold of the chandeliers so that he seemed half-man, half-omen — a raven risen from the ashes of civility. The black lacquer caught every flicker of flame, turning the air around him to shadow and light. Beneath it, his eyes gleamed — cold, commanding, alive with the satisfaction of being both feared and admired. It was not a costume, but a coronation; the room seemed to bow before him without ever meaning to.

He laughed, low and deliberate, each note of it coiling like a chain through the room. Faces bent toward him, eager, complicit. Men of Parliament, lords, merchants — I caught fragments of names whispered about me, names I had heard in papers, names that commanded ships, factories, and towns. They were all here, all drawn into his orbit like moths about flame.

I pressed closer to Alaric, my pulse racing so hard I feared it would shake the mask from my face. He felt it — of course he felt it — and subtly turned, interposing himself between me and the path Edmund cut through the throng.

Still, I looked for answers. I searched every alcove, every corner where shadows might conceal what I must know. My heart ached with the weight of it — the splendour, the ruin, the knowledge that beneath all this silk and candlelight lay shackles. I was a stranger in their masquerade, cloaked in finery yet captive all the same.

And if Edmund's eyes should find mine, then God help me.

❖

The violins quickened, a reel unfurling like ribbons in the air, drawing masked figures to the floor. The chamber filled with motion — silks swirling, feathers trembling, jewels glinting in candlelight. Yet even amidst such splendour, I could not shed the suffocating weight of Edmund's presence. His laughter rang too loudly, too rich, threading itself through the music until the very walls seemed to echo.

I clung to Alaric's arm as we strode further into the throng, our steps measured, deliberate. The eyes of the assembly followed us still — two figures bound together where one had always stood alone. I could feel their whispers coil and hiss behind masks and fans: Who is she? Has the shadowed master taken a bride?

Alaric's hand tightened over mine, steady, though his own mask of composure was taut. He inclined his head slightly, whispering close so only I could hear.

"Do not falter. They will see fear before they see your face."

I swallowed hard, drawing my spine straight.

"And what if Edmund sees both?"

His eyes — dark, resolute — met mine through the narrow slit of his mask.

"Then I will see him blind."

The words steadied me, though only faintly. My gaze wandered across the faces that swam around us, each one hidden, each one strange. There were gentlemen of parliament, their familiar voices betrayed beneath gaudy disguises. There were merchants' wives, their jewels too heavy for their frail necks, fluttering like birds caught in a gilded snare. Even clergymen stood among them, robes concealed beneath cloaks, their hands not folded in prayer but wrapped around goblets of wine.

And everywhere — everywhere — the women. The women from below. They spilled onto the floor like living flame, the dancers from the brothel — half-naked, though they glittered with more jewels than any duchess. Their torsos were bare save for the chains that draped them, gold and silver kissing their skin, strands dangling with gems that caught the candlelight and pointed downward, winking cruelly at their navel.

They clung to the men as though drowning, pressing close, their bodies winding serpentine around broad shoulders and silken waistcoats.

Around their hips shimmered sarongs of peacock feathers, stitched into the skirts that glowed liquid emerald. Each plume shimmered with an iridescent eye, green shifting to sapphire, to bronze, as if the feathers themselves breathed with the light. The movement of their hips sent the skirts rippling, a storm of eyes watching from every angle — dazzling, mocking, impossible to look away from.

The men drank it in — eyes glassy with lust, mouths slack with laughter too loud for the hour. Fingers slipped over hips and breasts with the careless entitlement of those who had never been denied. The hall smelled of sweat and perfume, a sweetness gone sour, as jewels clattered like coins upon flesh.

Some whisper that piskies lead men astray on the moors. But men do not need fairies to ruin themselves — they have greed enough for that—greed like a tide, swelling and spilling, unashamed.

And the women? The wives of these wolves stood at the edges, their jewels dimmer, their silks tighter, their eyes wide and unblinking. Some joined in, compelled by expectation, wearing smiles as thin as glass. Others stood back in silence, as though their stillness itself were a kind of duty. Here, a woman's choice was no choice at all: to comply or to simply vanish. To be touched, or to be invisible.

I thought then of how women are taught to be small — to fold their ambitions like serviettes, to present a pretty edge and be content to be passed over. The women who vanish into their husband's names, like rivers swallowed by the sea. In parlours and papers, they write of virtue and duty; in the back rooms of houses like Marrowhall and in the hush of country manors they keep a separate ledger — one that measures the price of silence.

I knew the dancers not by name, but by their eyes: hollow, glittering with forced gaiety, their smiles thin as paper. Their masks were painted, feathered, adorned to make them alluring — yet the sorrow bled through regardless, a truth no satin could veil. Some were led on chains of arms by men twice their age; others drifted like spectres, pale beneath rouge.

My stomach turned. I wanted to cry out, to demand the music halt, that the chandeliers be torn down and the chains broken. Yet I could not. I was but one of the lambs amongst the wolves, and my only shield was the mask upon my face.

"Drink?" A man appeared at my elbow, his mask the gleam of gold, his smile predatory. He held a glass of wine aloft, lowering his voice as he added, "No mask can hide such fire in the eyes."

Before I could speak, Alaric shifted, his presence dark as thunder. "She does not drink."

The man faltered beneath his stare, muttered some apology, and vanished into the crowd.

I let out the breath I had not realised I held.

"They circle," I whispered.

"They will circle until Edmund directs them elsewhere," Alaric murmured. His jaw was set, his hand warm upon mine. "Do not fear — he shouldn't suspect you tonight. Not unless you give yourself away."

But even as he spoke, I felt Edmunds presence press further. I could see him, flanked by his newly chosen women, each draped in crimson gauze; shepherding them around like cattle in an auction. His cigar smoked languidly, and with every step proclaiming ownership. He spoke to no one yet, but every head turned to him as if drawn by gravity itself.

I froze, my nails digging into Alaric's sleeve.

"Compose yourself Alex," Alaric breathed.

Yet as Edmund pressed into the crowd, his gaze raked across each face. I dared not lower my head too swiftly, for it might betray me. Instead, I forced my chin aloft, as though I were but another guest admiring the chandeliers.

Still — I felt it. The graze of his gaze.

The wolf's eyes, hunting, pausing.

Alaric moved subtly, placing himself again between us, a shadow shielding me. The gesture steadied me, but also confirmed the dread blooming in my chest: Edmund had not recognised me—but his instincts had stirred; a predator sensing prey.

The violins swelled. Masks glittered. The masquerade whirled on, a storm of colour and deceit. But beneath it all, the game had begun.

❖

As we stood amongst the swarm, the dancers surged forward, their jewels flashing, their fans fluttering in a storm of colour. They pressed close, circling Alaric as though he were some rare prize returned from exile. Laughter pealed too loudly; gloved fingers lingered too boldly. Their perfume filled the air, heady and sweet, suffocating. I watched their lips bend near his ear, their hands brush his sleeve- watched as his tall frame grew rigid. Yet his eyes sought me still, across the sea of masks.

But I too was not spared.

"Ah, a vision!" one mask declared, bowing low before me with his horns. His mask gleamed gold, his voice thick with wine. "Surely you are no stranger to admiration, my lady?"

Another joined him at once, tall, with a voice smooth as velvet: "But admiration is too mild a word for such beauty." His gaze lingered on the curve of my gown, bold enough to make my blood chill.

I moved to step aside, but a third blocked my path, his grin too wide. "Do not vanish so soon, little dove. The night is young, and so are you."

Their words pressed upon me — stripping away the mask's fragile protection. I was a helpless fox cornered by hounds.

One seized my hand, bowing too low, holding too long. Another leaned close enough that I felt the heat of his breath against my cheek. That is when true panic rose sharp in my throat. I glanced for Alaric, but he was still ensnared, besieged by women whose laughter rang like bells of mockery. His shoulders stiffened, his jaw taut- he was breaking under their clamour, yet the distance between us stretched like an unbridgeable sea, the sea of Hades' doomed souls.

The men pressed even closer and my heart thundered so violently I feared it might betray me. Their laughter grew sharper, their remarks bolder, their bodies too close, hemming me in. The chamber, with its gilded walls and glittering chandeliers, became a cage, the music a taunt.

One bent near, his voice low, almost a growl.

"Tell me, little mask, who claims you this night?"

For a heartbeat I could not breathe.

But then — across the sea of feathers and silks, across the smothering press of hands and voices — I saw him.

Edmund. Watching me.

Not with surprise, nor recognition of one stumbled upon by chance, but with the slow, deliberate study of a predator who has tracked his kill all along. His cigar burned between his fingers, the smoke curling upward like a signal of conquest. His mask of black velvet revealed the cruel curl of his mouth, the arrogance carved into his jaw. And when his eyes caught mine — those eyes shaped just as Alaric's, yet void of all gentleness — my blood turned to ice.

He grinned — then he began to move toward me.

The crowd parted of its own accord, laughter softening to murmurs, as though some instinct warned them of what approached. My breath faltered, my pulse hammering against my ribs. The men around me fell back, cowed by a force greater than their bravado.

Edmund Rothwell crossed the floor with the ease of a man who believes the world itself belongs to him. Step by step, closer, his gaze never breaking from mine.

I felt the walls close in, the music twist to a discordant echo. My mask concealed me, yet I knew with dreadful certainty: if he reached me, no disguise in the world would save me.

The wolf had scented the lamb.

Before time allowed me to gather myself, Edmund stood before us like a dark idol; his cigar smouldering in the air between us, its smoke curling into my mask as though it would suffocate me. The violins faltered, caught, then resumed, but I heard little of them — only the thunder of my heart, the sickly sweetness of wine, and Edmund's voice as it unfurled in a mockery of charm.

"And who," he drawled, his words cutting through laughter and chatter alike, "is this ravishing creature?" His eyes, gleaming predator's eyes, raked over me with deliberate slowness, every inch of his gaze a trespass. "Tell me, brother, is she your prize for the evening?"

A ripple of amusement ran through the onlookers. Fans snapped open; men chuckled into their goblets. The scent of perfume and smoke thickened, pressing me inward, until I wished the marble floor might open and swallow me whole.

I could not move. I dared not. The mask was my only salvation.

Edmund grimaced wider, revealing white teeth through the haze of smoke. He leaned nearer, so near that the heat of his cigar brushed against my skin. "She is too fine to keep to yourself, Alaric," he purred. "What sport is there in hoarding such a delight? Tell me—" his voice rose, cruel, coaxing the crowd into his game— "is she to be shared?"

Gasps, laughter, a flutter of silks. All eyes were upon me.

Alaric's hand tightened on mine until it nearly hurt. He did not flinch, though his jaw hardened, his shoulders tensed beneath the silk of his coat. When he spoke, it was smooth, deliberate, yet beneath the calm lay steel.

"She is with me tonight—*brother*," he said, every syllable cold as a blade. "And not one to be trifled with."

A silence shivered through the chamber, brief but palpable, before Edmund's laughter broke it — loud, triumphant, filling every corner of the hall. He clapped Alaric upon the shoulder with a brother's ease that was anything but fraternal.

"*With me*, he says!" Edmund howled, turning to the audience. "Hear it! Alaric, the ice-hearted recluse, claims a prize at last! Well, let us drink to it, friends. To beauty—in disguise!"

Glasses rose, crystal chimed. The company toasted, the violins swelled, and yet I stood trembling as though before a scaffold. Edmund's eyes returned to me. He prowled around us in a slow circle, exhaling smoke that coiled like a serpent between his lips. I felt his gaze burn through silk, through bone, into the very core of me.

Inside, my thoughts raced. Does he see me beneath this mask? Or does he merely suspect, and play this charade for his amusement?

When he stopped before me once more, he bent low, his words pitched for my ears alone though his smile was for the crowd.

"Careful, little dove," he murmured, the ember of his cigar flaring in the shadows. "A mask may hide the face— but not the fear."

My breath stifled.

Did he know? Or was he toying with me as a cat toys with a mouse, delaying the strike until terror itself was his feast? I dared not answer. I dared not move. But in that moment, as the music swirled and the company laughed and applauded, I felt the truth in my bones: Edmund was circling, and it was only a matter of time before I was exposed.

"To the ballroom" he sneered, and with an applaud to beckon his throngs. "Let's feast".

❖

The ballroom, just a stone's throw away from the gallery had been remade into a banquet hall — or rather, into a stage for cruelty. Where once chandeliers had cast their light over dance and guiltless jamboree, now a single long table stretched nearly the length of the chamber. Candles in heavy iron sconces burned low, dripping crimson wax onto the floor, their glow thick with smoke and shadow.

Upon the table, silver trays sagged beneath roasted meats, their fat glistening in the candlelight. Towers of glazed fruits leaned precariously, juices spilling like blood across the cloth. Sweetmeats, breads, and goblets of wine crowded every space. Yet the crowning horror lay in the centre — a woman stretched out and stripped bare upon the boards, her body strewn with grapes, slices of melon, and blossoms of roses. She was no guest, no reveller, but a platter upon which Edmund Rothwell displayed his dominion.

The company gasped — some nervously, some in admiration. Fans snapped open, masks tilted, voices buzzed with excitement laced with dread. None dared disobey when Edmund strode to the head of the table, cigar between his fingers, and gestured for all to sit.

"Come," he declared, his voice slicing through the music, "indulge yourselves. For what is life but appetite unchained?"

With a flourish, he *clicked his fingers*. Two masked men appeared at once, silent, efficient, and seized Alaric by the arms. He resisted, but their grip was iron. Edmund's smile gleamed.

"Sit my brother here," he said, indicating the chair directly next to his own, at the head of the table. "Let him see what generosity looks like."

They forced Alaric down into the high-backed chair, pinning his shoulders until his knuckles blanched on the armrests. His eyes burned across the distance, fixed on Edmund — and on me.

"And as for you, my little bird—" Edmund turned, his gaze locking onto me. He drew out a chair at his other side, and with a mockery of gallantry, guided me down into it. His hand lingered too long at my waist.

Before I could speak, before I could rise, a goblet was pressed into my hand. The wine within was dark, its surface glinting like ink. Edmund lifted his own cup and raised it high.

"To beauty. To hunger. To what the mask conceals — and what it reveals!"

A cheer rang out from the guests, and he tipped his goblet toward my lips.

"Drink," he ordered.

I hesitated. My pulse thundered.

Across the table, Alaric's voice cut like a whip. "Edmund—don't—"

But the guards shoved him back down.

Edmund's laughter followed. "What? Would you have me deny her the sweetness of the feast?"

The goblet tilted, and the liquid slid into my mouth. It burned as it went down — too sharp, too heavy, spiced with something unfamiliar. My head began to swim almost at once, a dull warmth spreading through my veins, softening my limbs.

"There," Edmund murmured, refilling my cup. "Another. One must drink to keep pace with the revels."

I shook my head, but his hand closed around mine, guiding the goblet again. The second swallow left the room spinning, the candle flames bleeding into one another. I clutched the table for balance, my breath shallow beneath the mask.

Around us, the feast erupted. Guests tore meat from bones, goblets clashed in toasts, dancers leapt onto benches to cavort with abandon. Yet all the while, Edmund kept his gaze fixed on me, one hand resting possessively on my leg beneath the table.

Alaric strained against his captors; his voice hoarse with rage. "Touch her again and I will—."

"Kill me?" Edmund smirked, his fingers tightening on my thigh. He licked the tips of those on his other palm — "Brother, you cannot even stand."

The company tittered, some nervously, others with cruel delight. Yet none looked directly at me, none at Alaric. Their eyes were trained on their plates, their cups, their laughter — for to intervene would be to invite Edmund's wrath.

At last, Edmund rose, drawing me to my feet with him. My body sagged against his, the wine heavy in my blood. He looked down the long table, meeting Alaric's blazing eyes across the sea of revellers.

"My friends," he called, lifting his goblet in a mock toast, "eat well, drink deep! For tonight, you may savour every delight. And I—" his arm swept around my waist, tightening — "I believe I shall take mine in private."

"No!" Alaric's voice thundered, shaking the air. He fought, the chair straining, the guards barely holding him.

A roar of approval answered him, though thin and uneasy. Edmund turned, lifting me as though I weighed nothing, and began to carry me toward the shadowed doors at the side of the chamber I tried to clamber from his arms; a moth caught fast in his web—fluttering, frantic, and utterly powerless.

The great doors closed with a heavy groan, and the music swelled again, covering the violence with gaiety. The feast continued, as though nothing had broken the revels.

Society bowed its head. And the wolf bore away his lamb.

Chapter Twenty-Seven

The side room was no mere antechamber. Edmund had chosen it well — draped in burgundy velvet, lit by tall beeswax tapers whose flames cast long, predatory shadows. A chaise longue sprawled near the hearth, upholstered in worn silk that smelled faintly of musk and smoke. It was a place meant not for comfort — but for performance, for power.

Edmund set Alexandra upon the chaise with a gentleness that mocked restraint. His hand lingered at her wrist, heavy as a manacle, and though his grip was not tight, she knew she could not pull away without consequence. Her breath faltered; her head swam from the laced wine, and the room tilted unnaturally, edges softening, gilded frames blurring into shadow.

"You tremble," he said at last, his voice low, amused, like a tutor remarking upon a child's weakness. He moved to the sideboard and poured another glass of wine, the crimson liquid catching the candlelight like blood.

"Do you know why I brought you here?"

She swallowed hard, fighting for clarity.

"To humiliate me."

His lips curved. "Ah, not so foolish as you look in that mask. Yes. To humiliate — but not only you." He stepped close, offered the glass, and when she shook her head, he pressed it insistently into her hand.

"Drink."

Her fingers trembled. She brought it to her lips, the bitter-sweet tang searing her throat. Edmund watched her drink, his eyes glittering over the rim of his own glass. Then, with sudden force, he set his goblet down and leaned close, his voice dark silk against her ear.

"You care for him — My brother."

Alexandra froze. Her mask was no shield; her very skin burned beneath his gaze.

"You think he can save you from me. From this house." He chuckled, and the sound curdled the air. "But I could end him tonight, right before your eyes — Shall I call for it? Two men, one blade, and Alaric would bleed out upon the tiles while you watched."

"No!" The word tore from her throat, hoarse, desperate. She half rose, clutching at his sleeve. "You will not—"

Her cry rang sharp in the chamber. Edmund smiled, slow and cruel, savouring the sound.

"Ah, there it is," he whispered. "That tone, that terror. Do you think he cannot hear you now, through those doors? Do you think he does not imagine me breaking you even as we speak?"

"Stop!" Her voice broke, shrill with panic. "Please —"

She wrenched against him, but he only laughed, withdrawing a pace, as though her struggle were a performance staged for his enjoyment.

Beyond the heavy doors, Alaric heard her cries.

He strained against the men who held him pinned to the chair, fury rising like fire in his chest. Her voice — breaking, pleading — was a knife turned in his gut tenfold. He could not see what passed within, but in his mind, he saw her torn from him, brutalized by the very brother he had long despised.

Inside, Edmund loomed above Alex, then he lifted her chin with the barest graze of his knuckle, forcing her to meet his gaze.

"That is all it takes," he murmured. "A threat. A whisper. And the mighty Alaric believes himself powerless, believes his precious Alexandra broken." His smile widened, cold and pitiless. "I do not need to harm you. I need only remind you both of what I could do."

Tears burned her eyes. Her chest heaved as though she had been running, yet still she stared back at him, refusing to yield fully to his cruelty.

He straightened, composed once more, and with calculated ease offered his arm as though escorting a lady at a ball.

"Come. We should not keep our guests hungry."

When she did not move, he tightened his tone, iron beneath silk.

"Stand."

Her limbs shook, but she obeyed. But as Alex rose, unsteady upon her feet, Edmund did not at once lead her back to the hall. Instead, he stepped before her, blocking the way, his eyes burning with a strange, fevered light.

"Tell me," He said, his voice low, trembling with the violence of suppressed fury. "Why him? Why Alaric — why not *me*?" He pierced a finger to his heart.

Alex clenched. The walls seemed to close in—She knew to answer carefully.

"Edmund—"

He caught her chin in his hand once more, not roughly, but with the merciless firmness of a man who would not be denied. His gaze bored into hers, his breath thick with smoke and wine.

"Was I not kind once?" His words fell rapid, unsteady, like stones dislodged from a cliff. "Did I not shield you when others would have scorned you? Did I not laugh with you, share with you—did you not look at me then as though I were worthy? So why not me now? Why always him?"

"I..." Her voice caught, fractured, no answer forming.

His grip tightened a fraction, desperation sharpening his tone.

"Say it. Choose me. Say I am the one you will stand beside — not him." He fired a finger at the door, "For if you do not—" His eyes flared, wild with menace.

"If you do not, then I swear I shall tear him apart before you, limb by limb, and make you watch. I will leave you with nothing but ash where your beloved once stood."

Her stomach turned to ice. She could not breathe, could not think — only saw Alaric in her mind's eye, bloodied, broken. The threat rang too true.

"Choose," Edmund demanded. "Choose, or he dies."

Her lips parted, trembling.

"I — I choose you." The words fell scarcely louder than a whisper, yet to her they sounded like the tolling of a funeral bell. For the first time that night, Edmund's expression softened. He released her chin, his smile slow and unsteady, like a victor tasting triumph but fearing it might dissolve on the tongue. The wolf drew back his fangs.

"There," he murmured. "You see? You always belonged to me." But when he offered his arm, she did not take it willingly. She laid her hand upon it as though weighted by chains; her body bowed beneath a choice that had broken her.

❖

Together, they returned to the hall.

The revelry continued — laughter, glasses clinking, music swirling like a fever dream. And yet all eyes turned, however briefly, when Edmund strode to his place at the head of the table with Alex tightly bound at his side. She moved like a ghost, her face pale, her gaze hollow. Even her shadow carried more weight than she did.

Alaric saw her then, and though fury roared in his veins, it was the look in her eyes that struck him dumb. Not defiance, not even fear — but resignation. A sacrifice made. A vow spoken under duress.

Edmund raised his glass. "Eat, drink, rejoice!" His voice rang out, a wolf's cry among the lambs. "For tonight, no bonds hold, no masks matter. Tonight, the world is mine."

And Alex, seated at his side, smiled faintly, a broken mimicry of joy — for she knew that by yielding, she had spared Alaric. But in yielding, she had surrendered something of herself that might never return.

The hall had soured with indulgence. Plates lay scattered, meat stripped to the bone, wine spilled like blood across the linen. The feast had become a carcass, and those gathered around it were vultures, drunk and laughing, picking at the scraps.

Alaric's eyes never left her. He rose again half from his seat, only to be forced back down by the hands still gripping his shoulders. His chest heaved, his gaze roving over her with frantic desperation — searching, studying, terrified of what marks Edmund might have left upon her.

And when he saw none, when she seemed whole, untouched, a sob broke free. Tears slid unchecked down his face; the relief too sharp, too cruel. He wept like a man reprieved from death, though the reprieve was only an illusion.

Alex did not meet his eyes. Her mask shadowed her face, and yet her silence was louder than any scream. She sat where Edmund directed her, her hand trembling as it lifted a goblet she did not want, her smile brittle as glass.

Edmund sprawled at the head of the table once more, his cigar glowing like the coal of some infernal fire. He raised his glass high, commanding the room with the ease of a tyrant whose every cruelty was met with applause.

"Drink, my friends! Tonight, the world has no chains!"

The guests obeyed, laughter swelling, masks tilting, the air heavy with sweat and smoke. But Alaric's gaze burned.

He watched the way her shoulders stiffened, the way her breath caught whenever Edmund's hand brushed hers. He could not bear it. His body strained against his captors, fury and grief tearing through him like a storm.

Suddenly, Edmund rose. He pulled Alex to her feet, his arm encircling her waist with a possessiveness that mocked restraint. Slowly, deliberately, he began to draw at the laces of her gown.

"No!" Alaric roared, surging upward, breaking free with the force of pure brute force and desperation. He vaulted across the table, scattering plates, sending goblets crashing to the floor. The crowd shrieked, some gasped, as he seized Edmund by the throat and drove him back against the chair. For one heartbeat, victory blazed. And then Edmund's hand flashed, silver glinting in the candlelight — a knife, pressed hard against Alaric's neck. The room fell still. Alex's scream split the silence, raw and ragged.

"Stop! Stop this madness!"

Edmund's smile was cold, cruel.

"One more step and he bleeds out at your feet."

"Please!" Alex cried, her hands outstretched, trembling. "I choose you, Edmund. Only let him live!"

The hall seemed to reel. Alaric froze, the knife biting his skin. His eyes sought hers, wide with disbelief, with betrayal.

"No," he whispered, his voice breaking. "Don't say it. Don't give him that."

But her words had already shattered the air.

"I choose him." Her voice was thin, hollow, a bell tolling the death of hope.

The knife lowered. Edmund's smile widened, triumphant. He pulled her close, his arm a chain, his hand splayed over her hip as though she were a prize claimed before all.

"There. You see? You are the little bird, and I have freed you from his talons." A hand stroked her cheek, as if brushing a broken wing.

Alaric fell to his knees. His hands gripped the edge of the table, knuckles white, tears streaking his face.

"Alex," he whispered, broken. "Please—I don't understand—."

But she did not move—did not look at him. Her eyes were hollow, her spirit shackled by the choice she had been forced to make. And all around them, the guests raised their glasses and drank as though nothing had changed, as though cruelty were a game and love a feast to be devoured. The music began again, violins sharp and fevered, drowning the sound of Alaric's sobs. And in the flicker of the candlelight, the night carried on — a masquerade of wolves and lambs, and one lamb bound to a wolf by shackles no eye could see.

Chapter Twenty-Eight

They led Alaric away with no haste, a gentleness that was all violence. I watched him go as though through glass: his shoulders bowing, the guards' hands at his wrists, the wet tracks on his cheeks like rivers under candlelight. He turned once—an imploring glance that tried to find me across the table—then the press of bodies swallowed him and the candles threw him into silhouette.

When I heard the door slam, time did something peculiar then: it lengthened, as if a great hand had drawn out every second and tied it to a thread. The violins that had been laughing a moment before suddenly stretched into a single, high note; the clink of glass became a slow, metallic heartbeat. The room — the faces, the silver, the ruined feast — moved in gentle frames, and I could watch each one as if through a reel made of misery.

I could see them all. The scavengers with their flushed cheeks and furtive hands. The women pinned to their chairs with paint and powder, leaning on elbows to watch the spectacle of their supposed betters. A maid with a cracked brow hiding a bruise beneath a feather. An aristocrat with a powdered nose who bit his lip so hard it glistened with blood. In that impossible slow of things, I read each face as a reflection of the world: want, shame, fear, the long accounting of a society that calls itself civilized while it tears itself to pieces at a banquet. They ate as if nothing had happened. They ate as if the world would always supply. Perhaps that is the cruelty of our age: the certainty of taking without consequence.

I could feel it all — the masks, the hush — as a pressure behind my ribs. My vision pulled close to my own silver goblet: the rim dented, a mote of wine trembling on its lip. The candle beside it guttered and threw grotesque shadows across the tablecloth.

I followed the path of a drop of spilt wine as though it were a pilgrimage: down the leaf-patterned damask, pooling at the edge, sliding to the floor to join other dark rivulets. Even the smallest thing was part of the great, slow cruelty here.

Alaric's face kept returning — imprinted like a seal upon my mind. I tried to fix him there, as one might press a flower between pages, praying time would not turn it to dust. The set of his jaw, the slope of his nose, the tremor at his mouth when he sought to smile but could not — I traced them inwardly, each detail a tether to reason. I knew then he was lost to me — that this would be the last moment my heart would recognise its own reflection.

So I carved him into memory, deep as scripture, so that when the rest of me was gone — he would remain.

He was my last fragment of sanity; my proof against the forgetting.

A memory then rose of something green and living: the meadow behind our childhood house, sun tilting and warm, daisies pushed into the weave of a braid. The world then had edges only where they were meant to be; the sky had been obscene in its generosity. It was a day where I counted the clouds. I felt the meadow. I felt its simple ledger: grass, sun, the honest murmur of insects. The past lodged in me like a sphere. It was a soft memory against this hard reality.

This country, these drawing rooms — we live in a theatre of decorum and decapitation; the one is only stage-dressing for the other. The chandeliers glitter to distract from the blood beneath the floorboards. Men trade women as tokens in their private games, and we, painted and pliant, learn to curtsey through the slaughter.

I used to believe goodness could anchor me — that a pure heart might outlast a poisoned world. But virtue is no armour here; it only gleams brighter as it's broken. I have become what I once pitied — a figure composed of silk and silence, a reflection designed to please its beholders. Not wicked, not fallen — only diminished. A flame blown out. I was now simply a mask upon masks.

Then I realised, the true tragedy here is not the cage I find myself in, but that I have learned to stand still while the curtain falls. Yet this is no show; there will be no curtain call, no applause, no flowers gathered for a performance well endured. When the lights dim, I will not go home to my family— for I am already part of the scenery, a part of the furniture.

A hand slid into mine—Tabitha's; warm, trembling, human.

I did not look — I only felt it, and in the cavern of my mind we walked together; to the cliff—to the waiting sea. The edge was clean, merciless. The wind filled our lungs. Below was nothing, and everything. We did not hesitate— Together we stepped out and the drop was endless.

I died inside myself and became silence.

A shell.

Though I sat among them, bore a smile and yielded to the strings fastened to me, what remained of my soul had already sunk; dragged, down, down, to the ocean's deepest dark, where memory cannot breathe.

Where no light could follow.

ACKNOWLEDGMENTS

To my partner, Bradley — thank you for being the one who believed I could, even when I was too tired to believe it myself. For supporting me through every chapter of this journey — writing while pregnant, writing postpartum, and all the moments in between. You endured endless films, historical documentaries, and more Victorian day trips than any man reasonably should — all in the name of research (and love). You gave me laughter when I needed it most, steadiness when I faltered, and a home I never have to fictionalise.

To my baby boy, Brody — you made me see the world with wonder again. I love you so much.

To my sister Olivia, my first reader, my second mind, and my forever friend — thank you for helping me shape these pages. And to all my sisters — for teaching me what it means to love, to argue, to grow into a woman with spine and softness both.

To the authors who first whispered to me through the dust of old shelves — Austen, the Brontës, Hardy, Keats, and Plath — you taught me that words can be rebellion, and beauty can be born of ache. And to Sarah J. Maas, who made me fall in love with reading all over again during my pregnancy — you reminded me that stories can save us, even when they break us first.

To my English Literature tutors — you know who you are — thank you for being the first to light a spark in me and fan it into something real.

To Jax, my cocker spaniel — for teaching me that love doesn't always need words. You've shown me that devotion lives in the quiet things: a paw on my knee, a head resting against my arm, the soft sigh of understanding that asks for nothing in return. Animals remind us what unconditional love truly looks like — constant, patient, and entirely without judgement.

To all the men I've read, watched, or known — the heroes, the villains, and the ones who blurred the line — thank you for showing me what a man should, and absolutely should not be.

And finally, to women — all women — because you are the heart of everything. You are the fire, the fight, the silence, the song. You deserve every story, every word, every ounce of recognition.

And to you, dear reader — thank you for believing in Alexandra's story, for walking beside her through death, rebirth and captivity. I hope somewhere within these pages, you found a piece of your own.

Printed in Dunstable, United Kingdom

71367998R00119